MVFOL

From Pemberley with Luck

Book 3 of the Highbury Variation

Corrie Garrett

Lanmon Books

MORGANTOWN, WV

Copyright © 2023 by Corrie Garrett.

All rights reserved. No part of this publication may be reproduced, distributed or transmitted in any form or by any means, including photocopying, recording, or other electronic or mechanical methods, without the prior written permission of the publisher, except in the case of brief quotations embodied in critical reviews and certain other noncommercial uses permitted by copyright law.

Lanmon Books
28 Amherst Rd.
Morgantown, WV 26505
www.corriegarrett.com

Publisher's Note: This is a work of fiction. Names, characters, places, and incidents are a product of the author's imagination. Locales and public names are sometimes used for atmospheric purposes. Any resemblance to actual people, living or dead, or to businesses, companies, events, institutions, or locales is completely coincidental.

Book Layout ©2017 BookDesignTemplates.com

From Pemberley with Luck/ Corrie Garrett. -- 1st ed.
ISBN 9798870453859

Previously in The Highbury Variation:

"Miss Crawford met Lizzy's eye, and they had a moment of silent communication. Miss Crawford's expression was bold and unapologetic, but there was a hint of self-consciousness. As if she knew, as on some level she must, that she had allowed the morals of London (or lack thereof) to harden and change her.

And there was a moment, Lizzy felt, when Miss Crawford might have confessed as much to her. Admitting as much to Edmund might have been impossible, but with Lizzy, who was sympathetic and neither her intended nor a clergyman nor a man... there was a moment.

Miss Crawford studied her, then took a shallow breath and rose. "But I must not keep you by boring on about my own affairs. I'm sure you have other calls to pay this afternoon."

Miss Crawford's poise was once again perfect."

–FROM LONDON WITH LOYALTY, BOOK 2 OF THE HIGHBURY VARIATION

{1}

MARY CRAWFORD WAS AN heiress, and her parents had kindly died young, leaving no expectations or burdens on her of a familial nature. She was also beautiful, poised, fashionable, and intelligent. There was really no earthly blessing that was not hers.

The only loyalty she felt was to her brother, who was currently making a great fool of himself, and had self-righteously told her to stay out of it.

She was taking him at his word, at least for now. Thus she found herself quite alone for the coming Season. To be alone was no bad thing, and if one had money, was probably the most enviable state. She had nothing to do but indulge her own pleasures and to look about and plan for her future happiness.

This plan included, firstly, a fine place to stay in the country during December or January. Most of the *ton* left London for country visits during those drear months, and Mary was always *en vogue.* Her current situation was becoming tiresome, and she wanted another option. *If* she had to stay in town, she would not be an object of pity—Mary Crawford was *never* an object of pity—but she did not intend to stay.

The second part of her plan included matrimony. Although being alone was the state to be most envied, a woman could not do it indefinitely. Mary had no desire to go back to her half-sister, Mrs. Grant, or her uncle the Admiral, who had settled his mistress in his house last year. A most improper arrangement with a woman who invariably crossed swords with Mary at every opportunity.

No, Mary would choose another place to stay, and one ought to choose from the very best.

Mary went up the steps to the Darcy townhouse on Gordon Street with the confident expectation of leaving with an invitation to Pemberley.

The late November afternoon was a little chill, but a wintry sunshine broke occasionally through the clouds, reminding one that even a little warmth was to be cherished. Mary's cherry-red pelisse, made of a warm, fur-lined velvet, provided comfort when the sun did not.

Really, one never needed to be cold unless one was poor.

She was shown up to the front parlor where the new Mrs. Darcy was just saying goodbye to another caller. Clearly the fates were aligned for Mary today, as she might hope for a private conversation with her. Fates often were aligned, when one took active steps to play the game.

The butler proceeded her into the room. "It's Miss Crawford to see you, ma'am."

"My dear Mrs. Darcy," Mary said, "I have not yet congratulated you since your marriage! Has it already been three months? How are you?"

"I'm well, thank you. Please, do sit and chat. We just returned to London a few weeks ago, and I have not yet caught up with all my friends."

Mary began to unbutton her pelisse. The first hurdle was passed. "And how did you find Pemberley? I believe you told me you had never been there before your wedding."

"No, I had not. It is quite lovely."

Mary unbuttoned her pelisse and made herself comfortable, spreading her skirts gently as she sat. The next hurdle was to get past the usual commonplace conversations. Mrs. Darcy could not invite *every* caller to Pemberley for Christmas. Mary must make a connection.

"You say Pemberley is quite lovely—which is true, of course!—but how did it *really* strike you? Do not fear to tell me, for I knew that you were making a love match from the outset. I will not accuse you of mercenary ambition."

Mrs. Darcy laughed. "Will you not? I nearly accuse *myself* of mercenary motives every time I come up the drive. The house is beautiful and well placed. The grounds are improved only so much as makes the natural beauty of the land more apparent and accessible. It has only been a few months, but I love it more than I could ever calculate."

"I am thrilled to hear it. My brother's estate, Everingham, is not as large, but I am very fond of it. I've never stayed there long enough for it to feel like home, unfortunately."

"Perhaps when he settles down."

"*If* he settles down," Mary said dryly. "You need not scruple to say so in my hearing; I know what the *ton* says of him. Speaking of which, society has rapidly forgiven you, Mrs. Darcy."

"You can call me Lizzy, if you please. I believe we were on such terms this summer. And yes, isn't it diverting? After my brief engagement to Mr. Knightley, everyone painted me as a scheming hussy, and I thought it would take longer to outface. They cast Emma Woodhouse in the role of savior, and Mr. Knightley *and* Mr. Darcy in the role of victim. They still gossip about me, but apparently the tide is shifting. Now I am an 'unconventional girl but not ill-bred.' I believe that is because Georgiana likes me, and I don't drape myself in diamonds."

A maid entered with a tray of small, crustless sandwiches and a tea service, setting it discreetly on the table next to Lizzy. The ladies took a moment to serve themselves a few tidbits, it being nearly four o'clock, the usual hour for tea.

Mary said all the usual thing in thanks, and the food *was* quite good. The cucumber was fresh, and the bread was very soft.

Mary began again. "You have brought out Miss Darcy this month. Is she enjoying herself?"

"Certainly."

"My brief impression of her is of timidity and reserve. I hope it will not be a trial for her."

"I'm sure you understand that I won't discuss my sister-in-law's possible trials with just anyone."

"But I am not just anyone—or, at least, I am determined not to be if you allow it. I really think that you and I ought to be friends. In fact, if circumstances had not intervened, I'm certain we *would* have been. This summer was full of turmoil, unfortunately, but I have decided to rectify what Providence let slide. I cannot expect *everything* to be done for me."

Lizzy smiled, though her eyes were still quizzical. "Sadly, I must inform you that you are not the only lady who has made that decision. I have my pick of bosom friends."

"Of course you do, for you married Mr. Darcy, and then he was kind enough to get injured in a duel! I know it was actually between Tom Bertram and Frank Churchill, but somehow society has made it about you and Darcy. Terribly romantic and exciting. I think it undid at least half the accusations against you because the *ton* loves a winner. However, none of that is why *I* want to be your friend. Indeed, I liked you before I knew you were even acquainted with Mr. Darcy."

Lizzy offered her another sandwich. "Mary—may I call you Mary?—you cannot gammon me. You taxed me with

Darcy's interest the first time we met! You had already correctly interpreted the situation. Three months of marriage have taught me to be a little more observant."

"Cynical, you mean, and that is a very good thing. You *must* suspect the worst in London, that is what all the best people do." Mary shook her head. "No, the reason you should trust *me* is that I don't need Mr. Darcy's money or patronage. It is a sad fact of life that wealth limits one's options."

"It is generally held to enlarge them."

"No, it makes the choices better, but it does not give you more of them. You must imagine all of society is a row of vendors selling sweets, and the more money you have, the more they pester you with caramels and candied ginger, demanding that you buy more."

Lizzy smiled. "This is a delicious, if chaotic metaphor."

"Thank you. In other words, you must find your friends somewhere other than the common market."

"Darcy has said something similar, but you need not fear for me. I may not be a *perfect* judge of human nature, but I am not helplessly naïve."

Mary gave her points for forthrightness. It was not often that Mary liked someone as instinctively as this. In fact, she judged that a little vulnerability might be the way forward. "To be honest, Lizzy, I do have an ulterior motive. The scandal between my family and the Bertrams has not died down as tidily as yours. It is nothing I cannot outface; however, it grows wearisome. I wonder if I might entreat a place at Pemberley for Christmas. I should love to be *away* for even a short time."

Lizzy raised a brow. "Your friends—the Van Allens—do you not wish to travel to the country with them?"

"I would, but they are not planning to go to Allenthorpe this year. They may have received other invitations; they have not mentioned details."

The truth was that Mr. Van Allen had been one of Mary's admirers before his marriage. She'd never seriously considered him, and he had not proposed to her. They had enjoyed a meaningless flirtation, and she had thought they both went their way as friends. But now, apparently, his wife's charms had begun to pall, and he was inclined to flirt with Mary instead. He would do far more than flirt if she wanted. It was childish and awkward.

Mary said nothing of this, but Lizzy's brow furrowed. "I'm not opposed to your company this Christmas, but do you not have other family with claims on you? Your uncle, your sister..."

Mary threw up a hand. "My uncle and his mistress are still making a spectacle of themselves at home and abroad, and my half-sister... let us just say that she is situated too near Mansfield Park for my comfort."

"Oh, of course. I didn't realize she lived so near." Lizzy considered her for a moment.

Mary hadn't felt nerves since she was twelve. She almost didn't recognize the fluttery, tightening feeling of uncertainty. Mary was supposed to control this conversation. Why did she feel as if Lizzy—a country miss with little experience of society—could see through her?

"If it isn't quite convenient, only say so. I daresay the Granthams or perhaps the Stornaways will hold large house parties as well." Even as she conversationally retreated, Mary couldn't help the slight manipulation. Of the two families she mentioned, both were known for their fast and scandalous behavior.

Lizzy smiled, as if she saw the manipulation, and was amused by it. "I think I would like to have you visit, Mary. Only let me check with my—my husband, and I will send you a note to confirm."

"You are too good, thank you! I do hope we shall be good friends. In that interest, I shall take myself off before you tire of me. The best friends are those you don't see too much."

She gracefully extricated herself, and when she reached the street, found herself blushing. When had she last blushed for her behavior? It had certainly been a long time. She resolutely pushed thoughts of Edmund away. These country people with their clear gazes and kind hearts would really be the death of her.

Lizzy changed in her own room for dinner that evening. She had not seen Darcy since the morning. He had been in the City for appointments, and then was pledged to Colonel Fitzwilliam at Boodle's Club.

She heard him enter his room while her maid was tidying her hair. His steps trod back and forth, and two thumps indicated when he took his riding boots off. After that she could not hear his steps, though the creak of his bureau and the low tones of his valet assured her he would soon be ready.

Lizzy's ladies' maid, a very superior female hired several months before, wore her black hair in a severely tight knot. Threads of silver enlivened her dark hair at the temples, and Lizzy suspected her hair must be quite curly, for the lady knew very well how to deal with Lizzy's curls. She usually did not smile as she worked, or ever, though Lizzy was beginning to understand her expressions. There was a softening of her eyes that indicated approval, and a twitch in her cheek just now that was the equivalent of a smile.

"Thank you, Clara. You are a wonder with my hair. I'm glad to see you in good cheer today."

"Nothing of the sort." She continued to fix Lizzy's ringlets and braid a small portion to tuck around the small knot at the back of her head.

"Nonsense, you are positively beaming."

Clara's eyes met hers in the mirror. "If you must know, ma'am, I received a letter from my nephew today."

"Aha! I knew there was something. You really must learn to control these raptures, one would think you the flightiest chit of a girl."

Clara's lips compressed to a line, though her cheek twitched. Lizzy smiled. She was certain that Clara did not mind her teasing.

"I stopped several of the housemaids from gossiping about you, ma'am," Clara added. "It was the same old trash."

"Ah. That Jane and I entrapped men of wealth? Was it the version where Emma forcibly kicked me out of Highbury to save Mr. Knightley from my clutches? Or was it the version in which I cast Mr. Knightley aside when I realized his fortune was almost nothing compared to Mr. Darcy's?"

Clara compressed her lips. "I don't listen to gossip; I stop it."

"Thank you, Clara, you are very good and very loyal." Clara nodded and slipped away when she was done.

Lizzy knocked on Darcy's door.

"Come in. That'll be all," he said to his valet.

His room was darker than hers, with wood panels on two walls, and striped paper on the other walls that was a dark shade of blue with thin gray stripes. He'd only lit a single candle for his toilette, so the room was rather dim. It was dominated by the large four-poster bed across from the window.

"I apologize for my lateness," Darcy said. He was leaning over his washbasin, his face dripping. Lizzy handed him a small towel to dry himself, and he pressed it to his face. "Thank you."

"It is fine, you told me you might be out all day."

He stood up and rubbed his neck, getting all the errant droplets. He was such a handsome man, so tall and good. Sometimes Lizzy still felt shock that she was married to him. At other times, it seemed the most natural thing in the world.

"Did you have something to ask me?" Darcy said. "Or are you merely hurrying me along for dinner?" He was almost dressed. He wrapped a white cravat around his neck, twisting it just so to tie it as he wanted.

"Oh no, you made me forget. What *was* I going to ask you? Tell me about your day while I remember."

He smiled at her in the mirror as he knotted his cravat in the subdued stye called the *triple-cross*. "Nothing very interesting. Paperwork with my bank in the city, a ride with my cousin, and a consultation with Mr. Bertram at the club."

"Tom Bertram! Did he bring Jane with him?"

"No, not this time. It was just a flying trip to settle a matter his father asked him to look into."

Lizzy sighed. "They've only been married a few weeks—and he has already left her alone? I hoped to see her." Jane Fairfax had spent the previous summer in London as a governess. When Frank Churchill made a vulgar and heartless bet that he could get her back, she'd come under much unwanted attention. It seemed half the dandies and loose-lipped fellows in London knew who she was; she'd even received several *slips on the shoulder*—terribly improper offers. It was regrettable, but it *had* made Tom Bertram realize he loved her. Lizzy could almost forgive Frank Churchill for it.

"Don't judge them, my dear. Tom was as eager to get back to Mansfield Park as you could wish. I had to cut off several reminisces on Jane's perfection."

"Oh, why did you cut him off? I want to hear it. You really must learn to listen to such things so that you can repeat them to me."

"Didn't you receive a letter from her only a few days ago?"

"Yes, but that is not at *all* the same as hearing what Mr. Bertram says of their marriage."

He had finished his cravat. He turned to her, tucking a piece of hair behind her ear. "You overestimate our intimacy. He did not speak of their marriage. He only spoke of the perfect friendship between Jane and his cousin Fanny, who I gather also lives at Mansfield."

Lizzy smiled. "Nothing about Jane's beauty or goodness or patience? I am disappointed."

Mr. Darcy shrugged. "I'd rather talk about your beauty and goodness and patience." His hand cupped her cheek and Lizzy leaned into it. Darcy was never shy, but he had a great deal of reserve, and it was only slowly dropping away.

He leaned forward to kiss her, and Lizzy met him halfway. If her toes curled in her slippers, that was her own business, and at least he had the decency to look properly dazed and unfocused when Lizzy pulled away.

"I remember!" she said. "I remember what I was going to ask you."

"Why is it that you think so clearly just when I am not thinking at all?" He swayed toward her, but Lizzy put up her hand.

"Later, my dear Mr. Darcy, later. Let us go down and eat. I will tell you what I have done, and you can tell me if I am wrong."

He tucked her hand in his arm. "Very well, what is it?"

"I invited Mary Crawford to spend Christmas at Pemberley with our house party."

"Mary Crawford? Are you and she friends? I thought she was very close with Caroline Bingley."

"She was, or is, but I thought we made a connection this summer. I did not intend to ask her, but she... she wanted it very much."

He frowned as they descended the stairs to the first floor. "You mustn't yield to every request or pushing suggestion. I suppose it can be difficult for someone with as soft a heart as yours—"

"As opposed to your heart of stone? I still intended to say no, for she is known as a flirt and rather *fast.* However, as we spoke, underneath her poise and wit, I sensed that she is reaching for something... better. You know her brother is still mixed up in scandal, her uncle is a shameless old *roué.* Her older sister lives very near the family that she wishes to avoid."

"Surely she has other friends she might go to. She barely knows you, and me not at all. She is not the sort of person I want Georgiana to be intimate with."

"I do understand that, and if you wish me to gracefully uninvite her, I will. However, I am not sure she *does* have any wholesome family to stay with. If she did want to improve, if her morals were undergoing change, where would she go? How would she avoid temptation? She is too proud to admit any such thing, but she might be—however obliquely—asking for help."

"You perceived all that in one conversation? It is uncanny."

"*Some* of us read between the lines."

"And yet you couldn't guess that I loved you?"

"That is very different. You are a cipher, my dear. *My* cipher."

He smiled as he pulled out her chair at the dining table. "Very well. Invite Miss Crawford. We shall see if your optimism in her is justified."

{ 2 }

NOVEMBER PASSED INTO December, and Mr. Darcy looked forward to returning to Pemberley. Georgiana was now *out* as the saying went, and it had not been nearly so traumatic as he had feared.

That was all due to Elizabeth. She bolstered Georgiana's confidence, distracted him from his cares, and made sure they had at least one evening at home every week. Colonel Fitzwilliam told him only a week ago that Lizzy had made more of a splash than Georgiana. "People like her," Fitz said, as they rode next to one another at Hyde Park, "or they dislike her, but everybody talks about her. The *ton* likes that."

"*Who* dislikes her?"

"That's not my point, Darcy. It's a good thing that your Lizzy sucks up the air in the room—it lets Georgiana fade into the background and only come forward when she's ready. Really, you could not have done better."

"I don't need you to tell me that."

"I daresay. There are still rumors about her "feud" with Mrs. Knightley—but if you have them up to your place for Christmas, that'll scotch that nonsense. Lizzy handles it just as she ought, too. Neither defensive nor bothered. Are you certain I shouldn't like her sisters? I like Jane, but I haven't met the others."

"Believe me, *no.*"

He sighed. "I suppose I ought to be glad. If they are as charming as Lizzy I should be tempted, and I do need a lady with some fortune. Speaking of fortunes, Lizzy told me she invited Miss Crawford to Pemberley. That's not on my account, is it?"

"No." Darcy looked up. "Should it be?"

"No, but my mother has been making comments lately about Harold and I. Your marriage has made her impatient of our 'dilly-dallying.' I wasn't sure if it was her hand at work."

"No, it wasn't. But if you like Miss Crawford..."

Fitz ignored that. "Did I tell you that Holbrook asked about Georgiana?"

"Adam Holbrook? I said hello to him at the Crimptons' ball the other day. He was two years behind me at Eton, I believe."

"Yes. He was under the impression that I'm Georgiana's guardian—which I am, of course—but I told him he'd need to speak to you. Might be just the thing for her."

"I'm not eager for Georgiana to wed at seventeen. She really has no need."

"That's true, but why don't you invite him to Pemberley anyway? It wouldn't hurt for them to become better acquainted. Invite a few other young gentlemen so it is not too particular."

"If I keep adding to the party at this rate, I shall have to build a temporary shelter to house them all."

"Ha—as if Pemberley could not house far more! I'm off."

Today Darcy went through his mail, methodically sorting and opening the personal letters first. There were several acceptances of his or Lizzy's invitation to Pemberley. Mr. and Mrs. Knightley would come. Lizzy's aunt and uncle, after several reassurances that they were wanted, would come along with their four children. Adam Holbrook accepted. He had danced twice with Georgiana at the most recent soiree.

Colonel Fitzwilliam would be there with his mother, Lady Matlock, his brother Harold, and his young sister Isabella, who was Georgiana's age.

It was already plenty to Darcy's mind—too much, in fact—but Lizzy had suggested that they ask at least one couple and one more gentleman to balance out their invitation to Mr. Holbrook.

Bingley would've come, of course, but he had decided to spend his first Christmas with Jane at Netherfield, near the Bennets. Darcy had been more than a little afraid that the entire Bennet and Bingley families might end up at Pemberley this winter, but Lizzy had reassured him.

"I don't say we shall never host my family," she'd said, "but the thought of it this winter, when I am still putting down rumors—well, my blood runs cold."

That afternoon, Darcy drove around to Gracechurch Street to pick up Georgiana.

He paused at the curb, and it was only a minute before she was out the door. She turned back just once to say goodbye to Lizzy's aunt, Mrs. Gardiner, a tall, refined lady who had become quite a favorite of theirs.

Mr. Darcy handed his reins to the groom who stood behind him. Darcy hopped down to the street to help Georgiana climb into the curricle.

Georgiana would have come at once, but another delay came as several of the children rushed to the door to squeeze her one last time.

Mrs. Gardiner cut this short. "It is not as if you will not see her next week at Pemberley, Maggie! You must not delay Miss Darcy." She gave an apologetic smile to Mr. Darcy as she corralled her children.

"We are not in a great rush," Darcy said. "But I am blocking part of the street, so we had better be going."

Georgiana finally extricated herself from the clinging hands of Bertie and Pip, the two littlest Gardiners. Darcy handed her into the curricle and climbed nimbly after her.

"They are such sweet children," Georgiana said. "I am so happy they are coming to stay with us."

"They are sweet, if you call it sweet to knock a ball into their neighbor's window and shatter it."

"That was not Bertie's fault at all! And nor do you think it; I see your smile."

"You're right, I like him. But Elizabeth says the girls get up to all sorts of pranks."

"Not pranks—jokes! And never mean-spirited. It is mainly Eleanor."

"Lizzy found a lizard in her bonnet."

"But I'm certain she did not mind; she is not afraid of anything. Eleanor asked me."

"*She* may not have minded, but it took refuge under *my* bed."

Georgiana choked on a laugh. "Oh, no! I am sorry. It did not occur to me that you might...that your doors are connected."

"From your apology, I gather you knew beforehand." Georgiana was a little old to be taking part in such pranks. However, she had had a lonely childhood, and Lizzy encouraged her. Perhaps Georgiana was making up for lost time and would put it behind her soon. "Just re-member, you might be a married lady in the next year or two."

Her mouth twisted. "I suppose so."

"I am far from rushing you," Darcy added. "You know Pemberley can be your home as long as you wish. Alt-hough, if the lizard situation is reprised, you may find yourself out on your ear."

Georgiana laughed. "I *am* sorry; I had no idea you were so opposed to the animal. I will be perfect. I promise."

Emma Knightley knelt by her father's chair, holding his hand. She was nearly scorched from the large fire next to her, but she was focused on Mr. Woodhouse. "I will be perfectly well, I promise," she said. "Mr. Knightley will take every care of me. You know he will!"

"But, my dear, to travel in winter... it is such an unpropitious time. Ice! Snow! You look flushed and feverish already. You will die on the road, and I will be miserable without you."

"I am only flushed from the fire, Father." She rose and moved to his other side, taking his other plump, pale hand. "The Westons will look in on you every day. Miss Bates will come for her usual Wednesday visits. I'm sure Mr. Elton will pop around to eat our delicious tea cakes. You will be right as rain. Before you know it, the two weeks will be gone, and we will be back. Then John and Isabella will visit with your grandchildren, and you will forget I ever took a trip."

Emma looked back at her husband. Mr. Knightley sat across from her father, one leg crossed neatly over the other. He looked a little concerned, but she knew it was only for her.

"You really must reconcile yourself, sir," Mr. Knightley said, gentle but firm. "No one would blame me more than myself if Emma took harm. But in the meantime, you must think of her. She will enjoy seeing another part of the country. Think of her pleasure at seeing Derbyshire and the views of the Peak District. That will inoculate you against the megrims while she is gone."

"I don't know that it will—but did you say inoculate? It is most odd you should bring that up, for my good doctor was only just telling me that everyone is using Jenner's cowpox vaccine these days. I cannot believe it! Even the Royal Academy of Physicians has approved it, and they have outlawed variolation. I do wonder if perhaps the cowpox vaccine could have saved Emma's dear mother."

"But Father, she did not die of smallpox."

He shook his head sadly. "One never knows how these things will take one; we do not know if it would have helped."

"Perhaps it would," Emma said, realizing this was not a battle to begin this evening. "I hope you will write to John and find out about receiving the inoculation."

"Do you think I ought? At my age, too? There are many considerations."

Mr. Knightley spoke up. "You might consult with Perry and Miss Bates. Perhaps you could even provide for some of the other citizens of Highbury who would not be able to afford it, otherwise. I would be happy to promote such a scheme with you."

Generally Emma and Mr. Knightley discouraged her father's more adventurous medical recommendations, so Mr. Woodhouse was surprised at their ready support. He could not but change his mind when faced with the sudden agreement, but Emma suspected he would come back around.

They were able to retire to their room at Hartfield without more than three more expostulations of warning, and only one expectation of death.

"That went better than I expected," Mr. Knightley said as they went up the stairs. They had bedrooms both at Donwell Abbey and at Hartfield, but they usually stayed with her father for his comfort.

Emma stopped Mr. Knightley with a slight tug on his hand. When he turned to her in question, she kissed his cheek. "Thank you for understanding. I cannot *imagine* navigating my father with anyone else. You are the most patient man alive."

He squeezed her hands. "You don't need to thank me. I would do anything for the both of you. And I don't know that I am so patient; I was done with the conversation half an hour ago."

"No, you are patient. You take the greatest care of him. Whatever did we do to deserve you?"

He dropped a kiss on her hair. "What makes you think you deserve me?"

Emma laughed. "Well, your humility in recent months has taken a tumble."

He laughed. "If it has, you have only yourself to look to for the cause. You must cease thanking me for every small thing."

"If I thought my compliments would corrupt you so quickly, I would refrain. We can really only do with one overweening ego in this marriage, and you have long assured me it is mine."

"Nonsense. You do not have an overweening ego; I cannot have said so."

"Not in so many words, but I recall more than a few mentions of my vanity and pride..."

"That was years ago. Acquit me."

Emma smiled. "Last week you said—"

Mr. Knightley kissed her to make her stop talking.

{3}

COLONEL FITZWILLIAM LIKED to talk, but he was nothing compared to his younger sister Isabella.

He picked her up from the Fitzwilliam townhouse next to Bedford Square, and though a smart wind was blowing, she did not stop talking the whole way to Hyde Park.

The wind cleared out the usual smell of London's smoke remarkably. Soon all he could smell was horses and moldering leaves. He turned in at the gates of Hyde Park, navigating the turn at a sufficiently sedate pace to avoid a dowager's landaulet, and the young gentleman in a high-perch phaeton who was trying to pass the slower carriage.

Safely on the cobbled street that went along the southern edge of Hyde Park, he looked again at his sister. Her voice sounded suspiciously raspy, and her cheeks were rather pink.

"I say, Izzy, you might be coming down with the sore throat that is going about. Perhaps you should stop talking."

"Nonsense. The wind is invigorating."

"Yes, you've already said that. I'm curious what you find less invigorating."

"Italian. Mother has decided I ought to learn it in addition to French."

"Why do you sound so woebegone? Isn't Italian a—what do you call it?—romance language? Isn't there a lot of poetry in Italian? Certainly all the operas are."

Isabella sighed as if she were a teacher whose prize student just displayed incalculable ignorance. "I told you a moment ago that I am currently devoted to the writing of *von Goethe*. He is *German.* If Mother was willing to let me learn German to read it in the original language, that would be something! But no, Italian is popular, and so she chooses Italian."

"Von Goe-tah?"

"Like most Englishmen, your accent is deplorable. Goethe is pronounced *goo-teh.*"

"If you learn some Italian, Mother will let you switch to German."

"I doubt it. I suppose I should not expect to find sympathy in her. As Goethe says, 'The soul that sees beauty may sometimes walk alone.'"

"Walk alone? What am I, then? I sympathized with you for a whole *twenty* minutes on the ride here."

"Making small noises and vague sounds of agreement is not sympathy. And you *laughed* when I said that my life is currently a plague to me."

"Well—"

Isabella eyed him darkly. "Goethe says, Nothing shows a man's character more than what he laughs at."

"That's not half-bad, actually, but if you keep saying '*Goethe says*' you're going to get pinched."

"You can't pinch me anymore, I'm not a child."

"You're twelve years younger than me, Izzy. You'll always be my baby sister."

In fact, it was she who pinched him. She was lucky he was a good driver, or he might have startled the horses.

"Don't be insufferable, Fitz." She winced as she swallowed. "Maybe I am getting sick."

"That's no good. We're supposed to go to Pemberley next week; I hope you won't be sick all Christmas." They were only halfway down the carriage road which ran parallel to Rotten Row. As soon as they were to the end, he would turn out at the Stanhope Gate and take her home again.

"As Goethe—fine, as *one poet* says, 'Classicism is health, romanticism is sickness.'"

"Just when I was forming a good opinion of that fellow...! Nonsense, Izzy, we'll get you home and you will rest and be well. In fact, you could rest your throat now and you'd breath less of this dampness."

Resting her throat was not, apparently, something she could do. He learned far more than he wanted about the German poet, and he told his mother of it later that evening at Lady Sefton's ball.

She sighed. "At least, my dear, be thankful that your sister has moved on from Shakespeare. From what I can gather, this German at least writes rather fewer insults and, er, *warm* passages than Shakespeare."

His mother, Lady Matlock by title, was a kind woman, who was quite pleased with her two sons Harold and Richard. Harold had inherited her late husband's lands and title. Richard was the hard-working younger son who had never given her a moment's grief, other than some natural alarm when he was on campaign fighting Napoleon's forces. Conversely, Fitz suspected that Isabella was just—the smallest bit—unnecessary to their mother. Lady Matlock was a kind and indulgent mother, but she and Isabella did not have much in common.

"Small comfort," he said. "At least Shakespeare was English."

"I know. I am not exactly *trying* to marry Isabella off this Season, but if she were to meet someone she liked, I certainly wouldn't *stop* her."

"No, indeed."

"Do you know if there will be any other young men at Pemberley?" she asked. "Harold told me that they invited several. Young Adam Holbrook, Harry Hawksley..."

"I think that is all. I suggested Adam as he might do very well for Georgiana."

"You two dunderheads cannot possibly be thinking of marrying Georgiana off *this* Season? She is far too young. And do not shake your head and tell me she is the same age as Isabella. It is not true, even if it is true."

"Now *you* sound like the German poet."

His mother poked him in the chest. "Go dance or do something useful with your evening instead of disrespecting your mother."

"As you wish."

She moved away to speak with other friends, and Colonel Fitzwilliam looked about him. The Seftons' ball was destined to be called a "right squeeze" at this rate. It was packed with elegant guests. The women were in colorful gowns, the men in various evening dress from red uniforms to black evening coats.

Darcy and Lizzy were here somewhere. He'd seen them dancing together earlier. It was not quite a scandal to dance with one's wife, but not exactly expected, either. Georgiana was dancing with Mr. Holbrook, and Isabella was dancing with young Harry Hawksley. He was a harmless youth.

Fitz saw another of the coming Christmas party and bowed to her. "Miss Crawford, how do you do this evening?"

She was a small woman, with black hair and black eyes that seemed to sparkle with animation. "Excellently well, Colonel, I thank you."

"I don't suppose you have a dance free for a new friend?"

"I've made a vow *only* to dance with new friends; to dance with old friends is *passé*!" She checked her dance card. "You are in luck, I have the next dance free. A waltz."

"But then what will I be at the next ball, or heaven forbid, at Pemberley? Will I be an old friend by that time, forsaken and betrayed?"

"Oh, no. A man never becomes an *old* friend until he has displeased me. All things are novel as long as they are pleasing, and all novelty is pleasing as long as it is new."

"I don't know if you've said something very clever or very obvious."

"The cleverest things are *always* obvious. That is why they take us by surprise."

Fitz laughed as he led her to the dance floor, and she smiled as well. "You are a good sport, Colonel, and you give as good as you get."

He enjoyed the dance immensely, for though Fitz was not a talker like his young sister, he enjoyed a lively chat. They twirled around the ballroom in the embrace of the waltz, and Miss Crawford and he meshed with perfect synchronicity.

She was not like his sister and her friends—whom Fitz was often duty bound to dance with—for she could carry on a witty conversation as well execute the dance steps.

He hadn't had this much fun with a woman since he first met Lizzy. And of course, he dared not even *approach* flirting with *her*, as Darcy was the best of good chaps but a little raw from falling in love.

The waltz was also the supper dance, so Fitz took Miss Crawford into the dining room where a vast buffet had been laid out for a midnight meal.

"Oh, there is my brother," Fitz said. "He is with your friend Mrs. Van Allen. Should we sit with them?"

"I have no objection."

"Harold looks half asleep already. Your poor friend probably needs company." Fitz pulled out a seat for Mary. "After you, Miss Crawford."

Fitz's brother Harold was in his mid-thirties, though he looked rather older from his habits of hard drinking, indulgent eating, and late nights. Mrs. Van Allen on the other hand, barely looked older than his sister Isabella. She had been quite a diamond of the previous Season, and was probably barely eighteen. She had rich brown eyes and hair, and a coquettish expression. She was also a little red in the cheeks, and there was a certain volume to her laughter that did not seem natural. She had been drinking a touch more than was good for her, perhaps.

Apparently Miss Crawford noticed this as well, for she did her best to subdue, distract, and protect her friend from her slight inebriation.

Fitz looked about for the young lady's husband. What was he thinking to let his wife get in such a way and he nowhere to be found?

Finally he saw Mr. Van Allen. He was not so young, but was a well-known rake who'd married the young debutante nearly fifteen years his junior. Mr. Van Allen was squiring a middle-aged lady with very brassy hair and a voluptuous figure barely contained in a white dress with rosettes. It would've been more appropriate dress and color for a woman half her age.

Mr. Van Allen had a hand on her back, and he leaned quite close to whisper something in her ear.

Fitz looked back to Mrs. Van Allen. She tilted up her chin and turned her head away, as if she had not seen her husband next to another woman. "Dear Mary, did you tell me you leave for Pemberley next week? I was ready to expire from jealousy, for everyone says it rivals Holcomb House, but do you know what, we received an invitation as well!"

"What?"

Mrs. Van Allen all but glared at her. "Yes! Are you not thrilled?"

"But you don't know Mrs. Darcy. Do you?"

"I've met her several times. She realized that I am friends with Isabella Fitzwilliam, and also friends with you, and so she invited us."

Miss Crawford's pretty face went hard. "I see."

"Yes, indeed," Mrs. Van Allen said. "I shall see you there as well, Colonel Fitzwilliam, will I not? I understand you are the joint guardian to Miss Darcy. She is the sweetest thing. To think I am only a year older than her, and already married."

Her eyes began to travel back toward her husband, but she drew them away.

Fitz upheld the conversation as best he could, but his attention was divided. There was an odd undercurrent to the air, and he did not know what it meant. Miss Crawford excused herself and from the corner of his eye, he watched her approach Mr. Van Allen and the female he was with.

Mary Crawford received the bad news as best she could. Why, oh why, had Lizzy invited the Van Allens?

To further ruin what had begun as a promising evening, now here was Mr. Van Allen making a spectacle of himself, his wife, and Mary. The voluptuous lady with him, the one straining her low-cut gown, was *not* a woman of good standing. Mary knew this because it so happened that the woman in question was the long-standing mistress of Mary's *uncle,* Admiral Crawford.

Mary was unfortunately very familiar with her and her ability to get what she wanted. She called herself Francine Frances—a fake name if ever Mary had heard one—and she had been on the stage at one time. Last year she had moved into the Admiral's house, effectively *ousting* Mary from the only home she'd had since childhood.

Mr. Van Allen was clearly flattering Francine. He even offered her a tiny cake, a delicately decorated petit four, and she ate it from his fingers. Mary was incensed with him. Even though the Van Allens had graciously—or not so graciously—invited her to stay with them, he had made the last month unpleasant for her. This had sunk him to a new level of degradation.

"Is my uncle here?" Mary quietly demanded of Francine. "I did not see him."

"La, my dear, no! He is not feeling the thing, but I said, 'My love, that's no reason *I* ought to miss.'"

The last thing Mary wanted was a vulgar scene. She smiled while she spoke. "*You* were not invited. I'm shocked that Lady Sefton hasn't given you the cut direct."

"Oh, she has, but she won't throw me out. Oh, a bit of the cutlet, yes, please!" She gave this direction to Mr. Van Allen, who was filling a plate.

"This is for me," he said, suddenly less amorous. "I trust you can select your own dinner."

Francine laughed. "Yes, just as well. Have you eaten, Mary? You are so slight, darling, you really ought to eat."

Mr. Van Allen stepped away from the table to stand next to Mary. This time he leaned close to her ear and whispered, "This is really your own fault, you know."

His breath tickled her ear and moved the curls that hung there. He brushed them back with his fingers. "I had to get your attention somehow. You've pushed me to desperate measures."

"By taking up with my—with—*her?*"

"You're no prude," said Francine, "you just like to pretend you are."

Mary turned away abruptly and went back to her own table, smiling as if nothing was wrong. There was no winning in such a public situation as this. She should not have approached them in the first place.

Colonel Fitzwilliam was still manfully trying to keep a conversation going with Mrs. Van Allen, who looked more flushed than before. Harold looked amused, and occasionally added a comment about Derbyshire, which seemed to be the topic of conversation.

Harold winked at her when she sat down next to him, across from Colonel Fitzwilliam.

"Good show," he said in a low voice to her. "Don't let the old broad get to you."

Mary smiled. "I never do, sir."

Colonel Fitzwilliam cast her a look of reproach.

Mary sighed. From his perspective, it must seem that she had abandoned her young friend to go flirt with Mr. Van Allen and then immediately flirt with Harold!

It was not at all the case, but Mary was done explaining herself to judgmental younger sons with high morals and self-righteous execution of them. Edmund had quite cured her of thinking such men were worthy of her time. They would always find her wanting, no matter what her motives.

Mary turned to Harold. "I hear you were at the duel with Mr. Darcy this summer. Now, please tell me all the details, and do *not* tell me women should not hear of such things! Instead tell me how Mr. Darcy ended up at the club instead of his bed."

"Ha, that was a bit of a thing. I've never seen my cousin so knackered."

Mary more or less ignored Colonel Fitzwilliam for the rest of dinner, though he did, at one point, speak to her alone.

"Will the Van Allens' presence at Pemberley be an inconvenience? Would you rather they did not come?"

She raised her chin. "Why would you think so? They are my dear friends. I'm sure it was most considerate of Mrs. Darcy to include them."

He only nodded. When Harold asked her to dance upon the return to the ballroom, she accepted with alacrity.

{4}

COLONEL FITZWILLIAM VISITED Darcy the following day. He walked into Darcy's study unannounced and flopped down on one of the chairs across from Darcy's large desk.

"Didn't expect to see you today," his cousin said, continuing to look over a letter of business. "I've the devil of a lot to do closing up here before we leave this morning. Did you need something?"

"Yes. *Why* are the Van Allens coming to Pemberley? Lizzy cannot know what she's gotten into."

Darcy looked up. "I invited them. Or rather, I asked her to extend them a note of invitation."

"But—Van Allen is a loose cannon, surely you know that! Not at all the sort to have around a cozy fireside with family and friends."

"Is he? I'm not as up on the latest society news as you. I'm acquainted with him, and he introduced his wife to me last week. She's friends with your sister Isabella, and also friends with Miss Crawford. I had the impression you were friends with him. I thought it made sense."

"I'm a little acquainted with both of them, but... oh, I suppose it's too late to rescind the invitation if they're leaving tomorrow. I just don't like Van Allen. He's already returned to his old ways and isn't making his wife very happy."

Darcy grimaced. "I didn't know. He didn't give me that impression."

"He probably won't make mischief at Pemberley. Perhaps it'll be a pleasant interlude for his wife."

Mary spent the last few days before her trip to Pemberley visiting many friends. In other words, she avoided the Van Allens' house as much as possible.

She would have to see them at Pemberley, but at least there would be many other people there. She considered removing with her trunk and her things to a more congenial location, but it would create talk. She knew her brief confrontation with Francine had been remarked upon, but thankfully Mr. Van Allen was not yet part of the gossip. If Mary suddenly removed from the Van Allen house, it would be noted. It would be a great piece of drama for no reason, particularly if they all met up at Pemberley three days later.

Mary found herself in an acquaintance's parlor this afternoon, listening to the debutante of the family play the harp. Mary's fingers itched for her own harp at Everingham. She quite loved music. The Van Allens did not have a harp at all, but perhaps the Darcy family would. They seemed the sort that would own an excellent instrument.

This young lady was proficient, but not accomplished. Perhaps in several more years she would be. It was a bit yawn-inducing.

The parlor was inexplicably papered with a hideous pale blue and deep pink wallpaper, and the several settees and divans were covered in a pink and yellow chintz that showed the same sartorial eye had been at work. Someday she would be mistress of her own establishment; then she could decorate as she liked. She certainly had the fortune for it.

Mary took another biscuit when the tray was passed by and nibbled it. She had a bit of passion for ginger biscuits.

There was polite applause as the young lady finished her song. There were five or six other visitors, including Colonel Fitzwilliam and another gentleman. The matron of the family smiled at them all. "Would anyone else like to play? Miss Crawford, perhaps?"

"No, not today, thank you! I am terribly out of practice." She would have dearly loved to play, but it would be stupid and impolite to make the lady's daughter look nohow by showing her up.

The instrument was allowed to be covered by a cloth again, and polite chitchat resumed.

Colonel Fitzwilliam sat down next to her in an empty place. "Tomorrow we'll be off to Pemberley. I hear you're to travel with my mother and sister."

"Yes, indeed. Lady Matlock was so kind as to invite me to share her carriage." Mary had made certain that there was opportunity and inclination for this invitation, and it had gone swimmingly. Mary was resigned to a few more awkward weeks with the Van Allens, but she certainly did not want to travel with them.

In fact, Mary was more than half considering pursuing Harold, Colonel Fitzwilliam's brother. She'd been acquainted with him for five years, and she was tired of being on the town without a proper place and home to retreat to. It would be pleasant to be his wife. *Mary Fitzwilliam, Countess of Matlock,* that sounded well. During the fiasco with Edmund, her heart had been quite unwisely put on the line and trampled. She was owed a good, prosperous, shallow marriage, was she not? She would treat herself to it if it came her way.

"I'll be riding along," Colonel Fitzwilliam said. "My mother doesn't often travel all the way to Pemberley, and she dislikes traveling without a man of the family. It takes at least three days, you know."

"Yes, so I understood."

"It won't be a very lively group at Pemberley. There'll be a few young people, but mostly it's family folk. Lizzy's aunt is bringing her four children."

"Delightful."

"Darcy keeps country hours. He's not much addicted to dancing or cards."

"And I am receiving this recital for what reason?"

"It merely occurred to me you might expect something different. Van Allen has always been a bit wild, and I know the Admiral moves in a pretty fast set."

Mary put the rest of the ginger biscuit in her mouth to avoid answering right away. Judgmental younger sons, indeed! When she swallowed, she said, "My uncle's behavior has as little do with *me,* as Lady Catherine's does to you." She had met his overbearing aunt on several occasions here in town.

He smiled reluctantly. "Touché. You still plan to go to Pemberley?"

"Yes, but if you press any harder, I shall begin to feel unwelcome."

He still looked troubled. His fine profile was somewhat marred by this. Mary didn't care. She was sick of gentlemen with fine feelings and intelligent eyes who looked vaguely troubled by her.

She excused herself and bid her hostess goodbye. It was nearly five in the evening, and Mr. Van Allen would still be at his club. Mrs. Van Allen would be napping before her visit to Almacks that evening.

Mary took a hackney back to their house and slipped up the three flights of stairs. She should've asked Fanny Price for tips on being mouse-like and unnoticed, for such things were not Mary's forte. In fact, though the thick burgundy carpet on the stairs muffled her steps, she must have made *some* noise, for Mr. Van Allen exited his chamber just as she reached the third level.

Her bedchamber was on the right of the stairway, his and Mrs. Van Allen's were on the left.

"Ah, Mary, there you are. Coming to Almacks with us tonight, aren't you?"

"I was planning on it, but I think I might have the headache." She stepped to the side to let him pass down the stairs, but he didn't. There was a look on his face that didn't bode well. "Go on, Van," she scolded. "Don't be an idiot."

Perhaps it was the use of his nickname, or perhaps it was nothing to do with her, but he was suddenly in her space. "Mary," he breathed. "Don't be like this."

She stepped away, collectedly. "You are determined to be the idiot, then. Isn't Alicia napping less than twenty paces from where we stand?"

"No. She isn't here."

That gave Mary some pause. "I thought she was. All the more of an idiot, then. If you want to break your marriage vows—though I expect you already did long since—find someone else. I'm no flower girl or opera singer."

"I know you're angry about Francine, but I was despairing."

"Go despair on someone else's shoulder."

"We could be discreet." He ran his hand down her arm, rubbing the velvet nap of her sleeve first one way and then the other. "You know better than anyone that the game is entirely in the details. Your uncle is a lusty fool, and your brother is not much better, but you're the one who said a little discretion would have saved him."

"I didn't mean—that doesn't make this *right*."

"Is it because you're friends with Alicia? You didn't even know her until I introduced you. She only invited you this year because I asked her to." His hand slid around her waist and pulled her closer.

Mary stepped out of his grasp again. "I may not have many morals, but I have more sense than this. You *know* a single woman can't do such a thing."

"Then marry some poor fool so that we are safe."

"Don't be disgusting. I don't *want* to be that sort of wife— Please. We are enacting a scene from a farce."

At Mansfield last year, Mary had done a scene very like this with Edmund in a play. *That* had been pleasurable and delicious, both because she liked him and because she'd known he'd compromised himself to even *pretend* to make love to her. Mary was finding the real scene less pleasant.

"Not a farce," Van Allen objected. "If anything, it would be a tragedy to miss this opportunity. I heard you crying after that parson from Mansfield left here. What does Bertram have that I don't? Forget about him. That's not who you are."

Mary grew ice cold at this invasion of her privacy and her pain. "You don't know me at all."

"Yes, I do." He kissed her cheek, landing more on her mouth than not, but then stepped away.

She wiped her mouth.

"You're having a fit of purity for some reason, but you'll soon grow tired of it. Did you forget all the snug parties we had at the Admiral's house? I know what makes you laugh, and I know what it tastes like to kiss you. I'll be here when you're tired of being cold and pure."

"I'm not pretending."

"Yes, you are." He whistled as he descended the stairs.

Mary presented herself bright and early at Matlock House. Her trunk was brought up by a carrier she'd hired, and she held her two finest bandboxes at her sides.

The butler showed her in at once and it was a scene of some chaos. Lady Matlock and Isabella were in an argument about—well, Mary did not quite understand *what* it was about—but clearly it was not helping the leave-taking process.

Still, it was eventually abandoned, and before noon, the party set out. There were two carriages—one for the ladies, the other for their things and their ladies' maids. Colonel Fitzwilliam was on his horse, and his brother Harold had decided to ride along with them.

This last change of plan pleased Mary. Perhaps her stars would align this Christmas after all.

Her conversation with Van yesterday could not but obtrude, as the carriage bumped gently through Piccadilly Circus toward the north road. She attempted to put it from her mind. Most gentlemen, in her experience, were subject to sudden fits of lust and folly and a woman must either enjoy it, make use of it, or make an escape. It was nothing to get worked up about.

Mary's heart whispered that she'd had to make no allowances for *Edmund*, but that was not a thought for a bright December morning. Too many thoughts of him led to regret. If she had not been so insulting of his vocation, if she had not been so cavalier about her brother's betrayal... No, she would not think of such humbling things today.

Even if Van Allen's fit of idiocy continued, Pemberley was not his home; he would not be so forward. She would simply *not* return to his house after Christmas.

The only thing that left her uneasy was the confidence with which he'd described her character. He was not altogether wrong. She would never succumb to *him*, but there would always be other men. Even after she married, whoever she married, there would be other men. Did she truly think she would avoid entanglement her whole life? That seemed ridiculous.

Perhaps he was right; perhaps she *was* pretending. Was she destined for that sordid end?

Edmund would be shocked and would soon coax her into seeing things his way. When he spoke, she actually *believed* his high standards were possible. He had filled her head with pure ideals and kindness and intelligence, and it was depressing when real life obtruded.

But she was not going to think of him!

The wheels bumped as they turned from a paved road to a cobbled one. The bell of St. Paul's distantly chimed twelve times for the noon hour. Mary smiled brightly at

Isabella, who sat across from her in the carriage, poring over a small blue-bound volume. "What are you reading?"

"It is a book by Goethe, a German *genius.*"

Lady Matlock sighed. "You have read it so many times. I brought *Pamela*, or *Waverley*?"

"No, thank you, and this is not his poetry, Mother. This is a new novel."

"I suppose that's better." Lady Matlock did not sound convinced.

Mary had a good head for memorization and recitation, and she did a great deal of reading, or at least listening—for her brother liked to read aloud. "I've listened to *Faust*; it will be all the rage soon. Mephistopheles is a delicious character."

"Oh! I have not found an English translation yet. You are so fortunate."

Lady Matlock leaned back into the corner of the carriage. "*You* are fortunate to have a friend who shares your interests."

Isabella ignored this. "Have you read this novel, *Wilhelm Meister's Apprenticeship?* It is about a young man who loves the stage. His mother arranged a puppet show when he was a boy, and it ignited a passion for theater in him."

"No, I haven't read it, but I'm fond of theater myself." She nearly told Isabella about the play they had practiced at Mansfield Park called *Lover's Vows.* Mary recollected, however, that Lady Matlock might not want Isabella introduced to a such a *warm* play. Mary wanted Isabella to like her, but not at the expense of Lady Matlock's displeasure. And thinking of the play made her think of Edmund and that made her cross, so she instantly stopped. "Have you ever been part of a theatrical?"

"No, but I should *dearly love* to. Do you think we could put one on at Pemberley? Mother, wouldn't it be delightful?"

"If you think your cousin Darcy would sanction a play, you cannot know him."

"Oh, pooh, I daresay Lizzy could talk him into it."

"Mrs. Darcy, dear."

"She told me I might call her Lizzy. Fitz and Darcy are so close, she is like a sister more than a cousin."

"Then perhaps you might call her Aunt Darcy—or even Elizabeth—but not *Lizzy*."

"Do you like her?" Mary asked.

Isabella nodded. "I did not at first, for she has a way of looking at me that makes me think she is laughing at me. However, I have learned that she merely loves to laugh. She also loves to read; she is the one who got me this novel!"

Lady Matlock sighed and closed her eyes, settling in for a nap. "I might have guessed."

Isabella leaned toward Mary. "Mother still doesn't like her. She thinks Darcy could have done better."

"Isabella, don't you dare say any such thing." Lady Matlock opened her eyes to protest. "It is my duty to welcome Mrs. Darcy and hope that she is worthy of the position she's gained. I shall certainly do so."

"Of course, Mother." Isabella was silent for a while, looking out the window to where the grim brick buildings of northern London were giving way to the gray, wasted landscape of the December countryside. The trees were blunted sticks, the fields full of gray dirt and stubble. A light misting of rain pebbled the window with tiny droplets.

Lady Matlock soon dropped off, and Isabella tapped the windowpane, watching the water coalesce into thin rivulets. "I think Mother hoped Mr. Darcy might marry *me,*" Isabella said. "Since he had already waited so long."

Mary wrinkled her nose. "Your cousin—and so much older than you! I know it is done, but I hope you don't regret it."

"Oh, it would be *ridiculous.* He is more like an uncle to me. I do like Lizzy more than I expected. I wonder if she *could* be persuaded to put on a theatrical. Would you ask her?"

"Oh—I don't know her as well as you! *You* must ask her—or, better yet, see if you can get Miss Darcy on your side. I bet that would do the trick."

"Good idea. You seem like the sort of lady who knows how to get her way."

Mary smiled. "I am exactly that sort of lady."

{5}

LIZZY WRAPPED A WOOL SHAWL firmly around her shoulders when the butler told her that the Fitzwilliam carriages were pulling up the drive to the house.

Darcy was out somewhere, so she was the one to descend and welcome the newest arrivals to Pemberley. She did not go outside, for it was misting again and quite cold. There were still plenty of cold gusts coming into the large entryway to make her glad for the shawl. The sun was already setting, for they were already at the shortest day of the year.

The three ladies entered first, followed soon by the two gentlemen, Colonel Fitzwilliam and Lord Matlock. There were greetings to be given, cloaks to be shaken off, and muddy boots to be dried. Meanwhile footmen brought in trunks and boxes and valises. There was a quite a litter of such things by the time the ladies and gentlemen were divested of their outerwear.

"I'm sure you are all cold and tired after three days of carriage travel," Lizzy said. "Tea will be ready directly."

"We ought to change first," Lady Matlock said. "Me in my carriage dress and Harold and Fitz spattered with mud—it is not right for a drawing room."

"The men's mud, yes, I'll allow that objection, but you and Miss Crawford and Miss Isabella are perfectly acceptable! Please don't stand on too much ceremony, ma'am, at least not yet. Only my aunt's family has arrived so far—none of the others—so this is still a family party."

Lady Matlock was a high stickler, but she was not immune to Lizzy's charm or to a desire for a hot fire and hot drink. "Very well. If Miss Crawford does not object to a little informality..."

Lizzy gave her a conspiratorial wink, and Mary felt a genuine smile grow. "I'm the last person in the world to object."

Soon the ladies were in one of the smaller drawing rooms of Pemberley, one that Lizzy and Georgiana had gotten in the habit of using. There was another round of greetings for Georgiana, and Lizzy introduced her aunt, Mrs. Gardiner, to the newcomers.

Lizzy had been a little worried that Lady Matlock would cut up stiff with her aunt, but if that was the case, her good breeding and easy manners hid it completely.

Relieved of this worry, at least for now, Lizzy could focus on being a good hostess.

"You make it look easy," Georgiana had told her several days ago. "My aunt thought that it would take you a long time to be comfortable hosting here."

"I wouldn't exactly relish a ducal visit, but in most ways it *is* easy. Remember, Georgiana, the job of a hostess is to make everyone feel welcomed, well fed, and comfortable. Whether they throw it away with bad humor or pettiness is not my fault."

Despite her sanguine philosophy, Lizzy *did* hope that her guests would have a good time. She and Darcy had added so many more invitations than they had originally planned; she hoped they had not created a bad mixture.

As case in point, her aunt's four children came into the room as tea was wrapping up, with large smiles and a mischievous look about them.

Mrs. Gardiner stood at once. "Now, Maggie, what are you about to bring your brothers and sister into the drawing room without leave? You know better."

Maggie did look a little self-conscious, and Mrs. Gardiner would have shuffled them out at once, but Georgiana intervened. "This is a good time for introductions, though, since they are here? I would like all my cousins to be acquainted."

This did cause Lady Matlock's nose to flare. Georgiana was placing Isabella Fitzwilliam, daughter of an earl, on par with four children of a *tradesman*. Lady Matlock subdued her ire with a deep breath.

Lizzy was never a coward, but she would be relieved if Darcy *returned soon.*

Georgiana placed a hand on the two young Gardiner boys. "These are Bertrand and Phillip—or Bertie and Pip. Pip turned six last week."

Both boys executed very acceptable bows, and Lady Matlock, who had a soft spot for boys, smiled at them.

"And these are Margaret and Eleanor," Georgiana said. "Allow me to introduce my aunt, Lady Matlock, my cousin, Miss Isabella Fitzwilliam, and our friend, Miss Crawford."

The girls curtseyed.

"Pleased to meet you, Lady Matlock," Maggie said. She was the eldest at eleven and often the spokesperson. "We *are* sorry to have interrupted, and we will not generally do so, but Miss Darcy promised to do a story with the boys before dinner. They were afraid she forgot. But now I see that it is because you have arrived, and we should not ask for her."

"Oh—I did forget," Georgiana said. "You will excuse me, won't you?"

Lady Matlock raised her eyebrows. "Don't ask me, dear Georgiana. It is Mrs. Darcy's place to excuse or not excuse you in her own home."

"Of course, Georgiana," Lizzy said. "We'll see you at dinner."

The children walked out sedately, but Lizzy could distinctly hear their steps change to running when they reached the stairs. There was a distant yell from one of the boys as they reached the next floor. Mrs. Gardiner winced at the sound. "I do apologize. They are lively children and so fond of Miss Darcy. So excited to be in a new place."

Lady Matlock's lips twitched. She appeared to be struggling between disapproval and indulgence, and with relief, Lizzy saw that indulgence was wining. Lady Matlock waved a hand. "I remember when Fitz and Harold were just that age—very dashing boys and very high spirits. Especially Fitz."

"What's that about me?" asked Colonel Fitzwilliam, entering the drawing room with his brother. He was now out of his sodden great coat and muddy boots. He wore evening dress—no longer a red coat, as he had sold out of the army—and he wore it well.

Lizzy breathed a sigh of relief. She liked Colonel Fitzwilliam excessively, and he was a social treasure. He was never ill at ease: always ready to contribute to a topic, encourage a quiet listener, or soothe a ruffled temper.

Darcy, love of her life, could not be compared to him socially.

The party, now encompassing six persons, naturally broke into smaller groups as Lizzy poured out more tea for the gentlemen. Colonel Fitzwilliam was at the heart of the other, and Lizzy was allowed to smile at her aunt.

"I suppose this is all going as well as could be expected," Lizzy said.

"Indeed." Another muffled yell from the schoolroom made Mrs. Gardiner close her eyes. "Please tell me my children are not always so loud."

"They are." Lizzy smiled at her look of chagrin. "Only you are used to it on Gracechurch Street because you are a very good mother. Don't let it bother you, or if that is too much to ask, keep in mind that this room is beneath the schoolroom, but we won't be using it much for the next two weeks. There are two larger drawing rooms at the front of the house, and when we have the full party, we will use those. They are not underneath the schoolroom."

"That *is* a relief." She sipped her tea with a sly look. "And to think I should live to hear you, my dear niece, choosing between your *three* elegant drawing rooms."

"And my own ballroom, easily the size of the Meryton Assembly rooms." Lizzy glanced sideways at Lady Matlock. "I had better refrain from such talk, however. As you know, some still suspect me of fortune-hunting."

"Oh, no, my dear. A *fortune-hunter* denotes a man. You can at worst be a grasping hussy."

Lizzy laughed out loud. "How dare you."

Her aunt's delicate lips twitched. "That is better. You can relax, my dear. You belong here. Your shoulders have grown so stiff you could balance a teacup on them."

"I know. I told Georgiana my philosophy of hosting, but I am not practicing what I preach."

"Now, tell me about this situation." Mrs. Gardiner nodded toward Miss Crawford and the two Fitzwilliam brothers. "Is something happening there?"

"Perhaps? If so, I greatly misunderstood Miss Crawford's reason for coming. I begin to think *everyone* is a better judge of character than I."

"It's good to be humbled sometimes. Gives one something to work toward."

Another muffled yell came from the schoolroom. Mrs. Gardiner rose to her feet. "Excuse me, I really must address *my* four sources of humility."

Mary Crawford had no experience of children. She and her brother were only a year apart in age, and she had no nieces, nephews, or young cousins.

She suspected her familiarity would be greatly increased in the coming two weeks. Already she had seen the Gardiner children twice, and now they were invited to linger in the drawing room after dinner.

Lady Matlock, whom Mary would've expected to be against such a plan, was as indulgent as the rest, and seemed to have taken a liking to Bertie, the bigger boy. He was pert and talkative, no shrinking back at all. He had a snub nose and round, red cheeks. He was probably exactly what a child should be.

Mary didn't *dislike* the children, but it was rather in the nature of having a goose or a—a donkey in the drawing room. She suspected they were not feral, but she didn't know what they would *do* either.

Eleanor sat down next to Mary without invitation and looked at her quietly for several moments out of the corner of her eyes.

"Good evening," Mary said.

"Good evening," Eleanor replied.

Mary shifted her weight, crossing her ankles beneath her seat. Eleanor did the same.

Mary reached for a book on the side table. Eleanor cast her eyes about and picked up a small pamphlet that lay nearby. It seemed to be a treatise on a new type of lime for farmers, but the little girl diligently studied its pages for some minutes.

When Mary rose to join a table for a game of whist, Eleanor rose, too. She drifted behind Mary.

"You have picked up an admirer," Lizzy said softly. "Eleanor is not usually so quiet and watchful."

Thankfully, Eleanor's flattering mimicry was no match for her boredom with the game of whist. She wandered off, and Mary released a rather large breath. It was amusing to have the little girl copy her, but also... unnerving. She supposed, at the very least, that four children were a decent buffer to Mr. Van Allen's stupid pursuit of her.

Mary was opposite Colonel Fitzwilliam, making them partners. He was affable and Mary was inclined to be in charity with him again. "Your whist playing is quite good, Colonel. I can forgive anything of a man who wins."

"If I couldn't exercise a little strategy and forethought, I'd be a pretty poor colonel."

"From what I have seen of the Navy, intelligence is only fourth on the list of requirements for an officer... if it even rates that high."

Lizzy scoffed at this, while she examined her cards. "No, no. That is severe. What would the other three be? I suppose wealth is one of them."

"Yes, of course. The second would be a fine profile, something that might look good on a coin, should they so distinguish themselves by dying in a particularly heroic fashion. The last quality would be... oh, I was going to make light of it, but I find I cannot! They must be adaptable. I do admire that skill. I myself take a *lamentable* amount of time to accept a foiled plan."

Harold was playing opposite to Lizzy. "If those're the criteria, Fitz got promoted despite the lack of a noble profile. Or intelligence."

Colonel Fitzwilliam rolled his eyes. "Your lack of brotherly loyalty would pain me deeply. However, I suspect you're fighting such a deep well-spring of joy to have me home safe, you can only express yourself in insults."

"You came home more quick-spoken than before, that's for certain. I think the precious army officers must've had a reading group or perhaps a toast club to polish up my little brother." He yawned and examined his cards with heavy eyes.

"We gave many a toast and a number of speeches. Most were not altogether coherent."

"I really think a young gentleman cannot claim a skill at all unless he can do it drunk. There is no practice in the world like doing an activity while foxed." Mary played a jack, tacking the trick.

Mary was joking, but Lizzy's startled glance made her laugh. "Not truly! You cannot take what I say seriously. I promise I have every moral fiber you could wish for. Some of them may have frayed, but they have not snapped, I promise."

Colonel Fitzwilliam made a small noise of disbelief. He coughed as if he hadn't meant it to be heard.

There was a brief silence around the table. Mary's face flushed, though whether with anger or embarrassment, she wasn't sure. She raised her chin. "It is easy to have a perfectly clean garment with every moral fiber precise and unfaded, if it is never used. A morality that is used and tested and washed is more useful, if less pristine."

All at once, they collectively realized that the four children had drawn near to watch the game again.

Lizzy turned to Pip and Bertie with a smile. "Is it bedtime? Goodnight, my dears." She kissed their cheeks and placed a hand on each of the girls' heads.

"Thank you again for inviting us," Bertie said. "It's bang up to stay in a giant house, and the Colonel says if it snows, he will show us a clear place to sled down the hill."

"That's right," Colonel Fitzwilliam said. "I will be the captain of that venture, and you my ready soldiers."

The boys grinned. "Thank you, Colonel Fitzwilliam!"

"No, no, I'm the captain now, remember? I shall be Captain Fitz, or when others are around, you may call me Uncle Fitz."

There was a small chorus of giggles and goodnights, and the children were gone.

The game resumed and the former conversation was tacitly agreed to be finished.

{6}

MAGGIE LAY IN THE LARGE BED with Eleanor next to her. There had been *two* hot bricks put under the mattress, and it was delightful.

"Cousin Lizzy has grown very rich, hasn't she?" Eleanor asked. "*So* rich."

"We should not talk about degrees of wealth," Maggie said. At age eleven, she was the most proper and demure of her siblings—except for perhaps Bertie when he wanted something, or Eleanor when she was pretending to be a lady. Eleanor could playact like anybody's business. She could be a pirate, a brigand, and a highwayman before breakfast, but when she wanted to be a lady, she was very good at it.

Maggie was the only one who was starting to be a lady in earnest, not in pretend. She was not so good at playacting and she rather liked the thrill of being the first to grow up and understand grown-up things.

"I like the Colonel," Maggie said. "He's been very kind to Mama and Papa, and to the boys. Not at all top-lofty like Papa was worried about. He said we could call him Uncle Fitz!"

"I like Miss Crawford," Eleanor said. "She is small and rather brown, like me. She is dainty and polite, but she has *energy,* I can tell. She likes to be doing things. I didn't know ladies could be like that."

"She is very pretty. Her hair curls perfectly, and the fabric of her dress was like lavender clouds."

They shared a very childlike giggle. Then, Eleanor went stiff as a log and sat up. "I have an idea. Oh, I have an excellent idea. It will be like one of our stories."

Maggie dragged her sister back down and pulled the covers up over their shoulders. "I don't want to do another play-show tomorrow. I told you."

"No, it is a thousand times better. A *real* story. Uncle Fitz is not so rich, is he? Not like his brother."

"We're *not* supposed to talk about degrees of wealth—"

"Oh, stow it," Eleanor said quite improperly. "The point is, Lord Matlock inherited the grand estate and became the earl. Uncle Fitz is a great gun, but he isn't so rich. I heard Mama and Cousin Lizzy saying that he needed to marry a lady with some fortune. You know who has a fortune? *Miss Crawford.*"

Maggie was momentarily struck dumb.

Eleanor poked her. "Well?"

"That *is* a good idea." Maggie tried to subdue the surge of jealousy she felt for her sister's brilliance, knowing the feeling to be unworthy. "And Uncle Fitz looked at her *so* intently during the card game. He likes her already!"

"Probably. She is very interesting looking."

"But this is not a game. I suppose we could watch and see if they have any true preference for each other, but—"

"There will be too many other people here," Eleanor said. "She has too many choices. There's Lord Matlock—"

"But he is so *old*."

"Grown-ups don't care about that." Eleanor casually disposed of such minor things as age and attraction with a wave of her hand. "Then there will be several other young men—I forget their names, except that once they arrive it is no longer a family party, and we cannot come into the drawing rooms without being summoned. My *point* is that we need to make sure she chooses Uncle Fitz."

Maggie found no great fault with this. Uncle Fitz needed a fortune, Miss Crawford had one. He was kind; she was beautiful. He had a family, she needed a family. "You're right. They would be perfect, but what are we to do? As soon as the other guests arrive, we will have to stay out of the way. We will hardly ever see them."

"Oh, pooh. He already promised to take Bertie sledding, and he was kind to Pip as well. There will be outdoor things they do with us. Plus there will be church, after supper times, morning teatime—we will see them plenty."

"But what would we *do*?"

Eleanor was silent for a while. The curtains of the bed frame had been pulled shut to prevent them from feeling a draught, and so it was very dark. Maggie could not see her little sister's face at all, though she could feel her breathing.

Finally Eleanor turned to her. "I do not *precisely* know, but I have some ideas. We shall have to be spontaneous."

"That's a very good word," Maggie said.

"I know." Eleanor yawned loudly.

Maggie was getting sleepy, too. "Let's figure it out tomorrow. How hard could it be?"

Georgiana still found it quite decadent and amazing that she could sleep in when she wanted. At the girls' school she had attended at Bath, there were standardized hours and a knocker. The knocker was the unlucky girl—usually being punished—who came along in the morning to knock on their doors and wake them up.

Georgiana also got to have chocolate to drink in her room. It was thick and bitter, but she was rather fond of it. It was another decadent thing about her life post-school.

She did not usually take advantage of her newly relaxed schedule as she generally breakfasted around nine with Lizzy anyway, but it was nice to know she could.

She was still in bed this morning. She'd put on her pink dressing gown and tucked it around her to keep out the chill. She sat against the pillows with her feet tucked warmly under her blanket and embroidered counterpane. It was quite cold outside, and she could see that frost had formed on the corners of her window. The ground was still stubbornly gray, however.

The Gardiner boys were desperately hoping for snow, but she was not at all certain that it would. Unfortunately, even in Derbyshire they were more likely to get rain in December than snow. Still, for their sakes, she hoped it would.

A knock came at her door, reminding her briefly of school. "Yes?"

Her cousin Isabella pushed the door open. "Here you are. I have had a wonderful idea."

"Have you? Come in," said Georgiana. "I hope you weren't waiting for me. I am late this morning."

"Don't get up, I'll join you." Isabella shut the door behind her and made herself comfortable on the bed. She took an extra pillow to lean on and bundled under the blanket with Georgiana. "How do you feel about theatricals?"

"Well... theatricals? We did one each year in school. It was supposed to teach us poise and elocution and graceful gestures."

"I am so jealous of your school years! I wish to heaven Mother had sent me to a school."

"It was not so pleasant as it sounds; rather lonely."

Isabella waved a hand with a faraway look in her eyes. "I would not have been lonely; I would have thrived in a crowd of my peers."

"Probably you would."

"*I* have never gotten to do a theatrical. I think we should do one. Here! Now!"

"They're very uncomfortable. There is much memorizing and—I am a wretched actor."

"I'll let you have a small part." Isabella was magnanimous. "But you must support it with your brother. He'll only agree if you want it."

"Lizzy—"

"Her too, of course, but she'll do it if you want to."

"I *don't* want to." Georgiana's time with the Gardiner children was paying off; she was finally learning to be forthright. "There will be other gentlemen here soon, and the thought of trying to playact in front of *them*..." She thought fleetingly of Harry Hawksley, and his sweet face and happy smile.

"Please? Oh, please? It would be wonderful fun, and I will not make you do anything you dislike. You can—oh, I know—you can paint a backdrop for us. I'm certain there must be a spare piece of wood about."

Isabella had hit on the only part of theater that Georgiana liked, the art.

Isabella sensed her advantage and pressed on. "We could even include the little children. You would like that, wouldn't you? I'm sure they would have a delightful time. They'll be relegated to the nursery, for the most part, you know, once the other guests arrive. But if we put on a show and give them sweet little roles, they'll get to be included!"

Georgiana wavered. "They would enjoy that excessively; they love to playact. Bertie and Eleanor are quite good at recitation as well."

"Perfect. Then you will support the idea."

"As long as you *truly* don't badger me to take a role. You must promise now, for I know what you are like."

Isabella grinned. "I like you better and better, cousin. Very well, I promise. I will let you be as meek and quiet as you want."

"Thank you."

"But I must say, if you like Harry Hawksley—"

"Isabella!"

"I know you do. It is useless to shake your head and look shocked. You must talk to him more. Mother says men like a quiet woman, but she married *years* ago. Modern men prefer a lively girl."

"I don't think I'm ever going to be a lively girl. Not like you."

"Nonsense. Darcy told Fitz, and Fitz told Mother, and Mother told me, about the *lizard.*"

"That was only—I knew Lizzy would also laugh!—it was for the children."

"*Still.* If there's a girl bold enough to hide a lizard in her sister-in-law's bonnet, there's a girl bold enough for anything."

Georgiana groaned.

"Your cup is empty but for the dregs. Goodness, it looks like mud. Let us go find breakfast."

{7}

Mr. Darcy served himself breakfast from the platters of cold beef and ham, boiled eggs, and fruit that were on the sideboard.

Lizzy had prepared the menu with the cook for the coming visit. With so many people in the house, more supplies had been laid in. If it did happen to snow, the roads would be bad, and it would take longer to get normal shipments from Lambton to the house.

"Why is your brow furrowed?" Lizzy asked him. No one else was currently in the breakfast room, which was blue and a little gloomy with the overcast light from outside. "The visit has only just begun. Nothing disastrous has happened. You cannot be regretting it yet."

"I am not; I was merely reflecting on the possibility of bad weather." He smiled. "But please let me know when I *am* allowed to start regretting it."

"I give you full leave to be sick of everyone in a week's time—I daresay I shall be as well—and then we will commiserate together for the final few days."

He dropped a kiss on her hair as he passed by. "An excellent plan."

Georgiana and Isabella were the next to arrive, followed soon by Mrs. Gardiner and Lady Matlock.

Darcy had been honest; he did not regret the house party. He liked most of these people, and he know how to be a good host. However, he was not used to having so many people in his home at once. For so many years it had been only he and Georgiana.

"We are expecting Mr. and Mrs. Knightley today, as well as the Van Allens," he told the ladies. "The gentlemen—Mr. Holbrook, Mr. Hawksley—will likely be here tomorrow. It was difficult to pin them down. As far as occupation today, I was going to take Harold and Fitz around for a ride. It's been over a year since they were at Pemberley, and I've some changes I want to show them. I would suggest that you all might join us, but it is bitterly cold. My man tells me they had to break up ice to work the water pump this morning."

Lady Matlock shivered. "We shall certainly not venture out in freezing weather. Some say the cold air is invigorating, but it is an unnecessary risk."

Lizzy placed the remains of her egg on the side of her plate. "Indoors certainly seems best for now. We have several chess sets, the library, of course, the music room—I'm sure we can find occupation enough."

Darcy became aware that Isabella was nudging Georgiana rather hard in the ribs.

There was a whispered conference, and then Isabella spoke up. "Georgiana and I were thinking it would be great fun to—to put on a small home theatrical! It would be delightful, wouldn't it, Georgiana?"

Georgiana looked uncertain. "I *think* it would be. We could let the children participate, if they wanted."

Darcy raised his eyebrows while he finished chewing his bite of beef. "A home theatrical? Aren't those very costly and excessive? I've no desire to turn any of the rooms into a stage or to outfit a company with medieval costumes and props."

"No, no," Isabella said. "We would not be doing it in *that* style, though I daresay, if Pemberley is like Matlock Park, there are some very fine old-fashioned clothes stored away here. We found a hoop-skirt in the attics once! No need for a stage, either, for I've noticed that in the ballroom there is a raised platform for musicians. It is only a step or so high, but what could be more simple?"

Lady Matlock's mouth thinned.

"You should be happy, Mother," Isabella added. "This would distract me from reading Goethe for the rest of the month."

"That *is* a point in favor," she admitted.

"What sort of play were you thinking of?" Lizzy asked. "I don't deny that my sisters and I have done a home theatrical now and again. It was great fun. We never had enough menfolk for the parts, but once my father declaimed as Hamlet. I think, my dear Mr. Darcy, if Georgiana and Isabella wish it, it would be an amusing diversion for them."

Darcy frowned. "But Holbrook and Hawksley will be here soon—not to mention the Van Allens and Mr. and Mrs. Knightley. I don't know that they would enjoy it."

"Emma would, I am certain," Lizzy said. "As long as it has a bit of romance, she will be invested."

"The gentlemen—" He looked significantly at Isabella and Georgiana. "Well, such things can easily lead to inappropriate behavior and familiarity."

Isabella gasped. "You, my own cousin, do not *trust* me?"

Lady Matlock put a hand over her eyes. "Do not be dramatic, Isabella, we have not agreed to a theatrical yet."

Isabella wiped the shocked look off her face and smiled sunnily at Darcy. "I daresay you do not know me well enough to know, but I am not at all interested in men. I am devoted to the written word."

"Er, well." Darcy felt the conversation had quite jumped its traces. His aunt had closed her eyes. "Even so," he said, "I don't think—"

Lizzy put her hand on his. "I do see your point, my dear, but if they chose an acceptable play and I supervise, it would not be so dangerous. I'm sure between Lady Matlock, my aunt, and myself, we could provide suitable chaperonage. Besides, unless I miss my guess, Georgiana does not mean to take a role at all."

"No, no," Georgiana agreed. "I might paint a background. I did so at school once..."

Darcy did feel better knowing Georgiana would not be one of the actresses. He looked at Lizzy. It *was* true that they would all be confined to the house for some time, particularly the ladies. He might escape now and again with Fitz and Harold and the other men, but she did not have that option. He did not have it in him to deny her an exciting activity.

"Very well," he said. "I've no other objections. We will need to use the ballroom on the 30th, if all goes well and we are able to have the ball as planned. Please don't make a terrible mess of it, for the servants' sake."

"Oh, thank you!" cried Isabella.

Even Georgiana looked pleased.

When Miss Crawford joined them a little later, Isabella filled her in with the rapidity born of true excitement.

The two ladies shared a wink, and Darcy frowned. Were they close? He felt wrong-footed already.

As he rose, he leaned close to Lizzy and whispered, "I very well *can* regret this already."

She only smiled and patted the hand that he'd set on her shoulder. "Go outside; it will do you good."

Mary Crawford was not at all sure *why* the Gardiner children had taken an interest in her. Currently she was bracketed on the couch by Eleanor and Bertie. Bertie was bouncing with excitement, and Eleanor, though not bouncing, was fidgeting. Sometimes she softly stroked the fabric of Miss Crawford's velvet dress, sometimes she sat on her hands, once she bit a thumbnail.

The flames were high in the fireplace for the footman had just added a log, and between the two small but warm bodies leaning on either side, Mary was a little overly warm.

She did not mind their high spirits or even the touching, but they all kept *looking* at her. Isabella and Lizzy were discussing what play might reasonably be put on, and with each suggestion, the children looked at her. With each play that was proposed or discarded, they examined her face. She could understand their excitement to be part of the play, but Isabella and Georgiana were owed the credit for that.

Mary extricated herself and moved toward the window. Even a few feet away she could feel the bracing cold that radiated from the windowpanes. It was a little after midday, and a thin film of sunlight permeated the clouds, but was too weak to offer the least warmth.

Maggie, the oldest girl, with curly brown hair that hung down her back over her warm pinafore, followed her. "But you will miss the decision-making, Miss Crawford! Isabella suggested *Much Ado About Nothing*. Would you like that?"

"Dear girl, it is not my decision to make. You had better direct your interest to Miss Isabella."

"But we want to make sure *you* enjoy it," Maggie said. "I am certain you are an excellent actor. You will participate, won't you?"

Mary realized that the other people in the party were looking towards her for an answer. "Oh, certainly. I will participate with all goodwill in whatever play is chosen. You need not cater to my specific tastes."

"Oh, good," Maggie said. "I'm sure we can coax some of the gentlemen to participate also. Probably not Mr. Darcy, but I'm sure Uncle Fitz will help."

Isabella was not bouncing on her cushion the way that little Bertie was, but she was excited. "If we do *Much Ado About Nothing,* I want to be Don John, or else Dogberry! They have the most interesting roles."

Lizzy looked uncertain. "I'm not certain about this play... it does have several inappropriate references. The one scene, you know, where the servant answers to Hero's name..."

"Oh, we will change that part," Isabella said. "We will only have her paramour kiss her hand or something completely innocent."

"It is also rather long," Lizzy said, "and contains more characters than we could comfortably provide."

Mary rubbed her arms, though she was still relishing the cold from the window. "We could cut the subplot with Don John's men. That would only leave seven or eight main roles. The children could be several of them—the priest, for instance, and we could even let Maggie or Eleanor play the maid you mentioned. That would make the scene sufficiently innocuous."

Lizzy laughed. "That it would! What do you say, Eleanor? Will you allow a man to kiss your hand?"

"Certainly! I will be the maid," Eleanor said. "Only she is supposed to look like her mistress, and I do not look like any of you."

Lizzy nodded gravely. "We will remind our audience at the beginning to suspend their disbelief."

"Very well. I should prefer to be a character with a *sword*, but I can submit to being a woman."

Mary smiled. "Well put, Eleanor. I have felt the same any time these ten years. Oh, to be a character with a sword."

There was further discussion as Isabella and Georgiana explained the plot to the children, giving a brief overview of the characters and scenes. They discussed among themselves who should play whom and how they might simplify. Mary offered the benefit of her experience, and Georgiana took a sheet of paper to make several tidy lists.

Mary was not much invested in the planning, but she wanted to make sure that she did not end up opposite Mr. Van Allen, if he should take a role when he arrived. That would undoubtedly encourage the man.

"The character of Beatrice has a great many lines," Isabella said. "Perhaps Miss Crawford would consent to play her? They are both witty and clever, and we really must have someone excellent to play the main female part of the play."

Mary was far from wanting all the attention of the lead role, though in the past it might have pleased her greatly. If *Edmund* were here to play Benedick, for example—

But no, she had put such thoughts aside. She ought to be considering how she might spend time with Harold, if she was serious about becoming the Countess of Matlock Park.

"I have no *objection* to the part," Mary said, "but I'm happy to let another take my place. Miss Isabella—you yourself—or even Mrs. Darcy—"

"Oh no, not me," Lizzy cried. "A small role would suit me, or none at all. As happy as I am to have a house party for Christmas, it does require a certain amount of planning. I would not have leisure for that amount of memorization, even if I was allowed to use notes."

Isabella shook her head also. "Not me! I am the director of the play and I will not have time."

"Very well, I'm happy to play Beatrice, if needed."

Before she could even broach who might play Benedick, the main foil and love interest to Beatrice, Eleanor piped up. "Uncle Fitz would be an excellent Benedick!"

"Oh, yes!" cried Maggie. "Let us put his name down."

"He may not wish to participate," Mary warned the girls. Where did their sudden enthusiasm for this role come from? She was reminded of the play at Mansfield—she could not help the comparison—and she shuddered at all the mischief that had come of that. "One of the other gentlemen might do—even Lord Matlock, perhaps."

Lady Matlock shook her head. "I doubt Harold will participate. You'd have more luck with Fitz."

"Yes, definitely Fitz," Isabella said. "I'll badger him into it, if needed. A sister is allowed to do that sort of thing.

He is just the sort of lively, quick-speaking man we'd need for Benedick."

The children cheered this determination.

Mary truly did not understand children. On the positive side, if the role was filled, they could not ask Mr. Van Allen or any of the other gentlemen to take it.

Some of the roles, it was decided, must wait until the other members of the party had arrived. The children were given their roles: Eleanor as the maid, Pip as a valet, Maggie as the nurse, and Bertie as Dogberry. That silly character was mostly cut, but Bertie insisted he could learn his very funny monologue and give it either in the middle or at the beginning as an introduction.

With this decided, the children took turns with Georgiana and Isabella and a very large printed edition of Shakespeare's comedies to track down the lines they would need to memorize.

This was chaotic enough, but it was exacerbated by Isabella, who could not decide which scenes they should do. She kept leaning over Georgiana and turning the pages back and forth to make up her mind. Georgiana bore this as patiently as she could, while she was also trying to copy out the children's lines.

Lady Matlock entered into the spirit of the thing, and discussed costuming ideas—the only part of the production that truly interested her—with Lizzy.

Lizzy, meanwhile, was trying to regulate her nieces and nephews, placate Isabella, and protect Georgiana simultaneously. Mrs. Gardiner joined the throng at some point, and at least pulled the littlest boy into her lap, but her efforts to quell the chaos were for nothing. Soon she subsided, and instead she and Lady Matlock discussed feathers and furbelows.

Mary found herself laughing at the happy madness of it all. It could not be denied that this was the wholesome domestic scene that every family imagined when they pictured holidays and theatricals. Mary had not had a large family—simply her brother and her uncle the Admiral. She could admit that there was something heart-warming about it.

She still had a smile on her face when several gentlemen entered the drawing room. Colonel Fitzwilliam was the first into the room, and when he met her eyes, his broke into a warm and happy smile that matched hers. It seemed instinctive to him.

Then he seemed to recollect himself. He turned away, saying hello to his mother and sister and making room for the other gentlemen.

The three men who'd been out riding still bore red cheeks and noses from the outdoor cold. There was slapping of knees and hands as they sought to get feeling back in their limbs. That was when Mary realized there was another couple with them. Mr. Van Allen and his wife had arrived just moments before.

Mary stopped smiling.

Lizzy rose to welcome the new guests, who were also pink-cheeked from the cold. Isabella embraced her friend Mrs. Van Allen and introduced her around.

"You'll be glad to know," Colonel Fitzwilliam told the little boys, "that it is starting to snow."

They dashed to the window, pressing chubby fingers and round cheeks to the glass to clear a spot in the condensation.

"The air is too cold, and the snow is too thin today," he continued, "but I think tomorrow, or the following day, might be perfect for a bit of play."

"Hurray! Captain Fitz!"

When the new guests had been seated, the children subdued, and the proper care and attention given to the Van Allens' journey, Isabella lost no time in confronting her brother about being their Benedick.

"Mary has already agreed to be Beatrice, and you would make a very good Benedick. Even the children agree."

"I don't know, Izzy. I haven't much a turn for acting." Colonel Fitzwilliam avoided looking at Mary.

"Nonsense," she said "You told me yourself that you don't mind Shakespeare's comedies. And Benedick is a funny character; no one could do him like you."

"Well, *obviously*," he agreed. "I am a droll and delightful fellow.

This made Bertie and Eleanor laugh.

"I still don't know that I want to be Benedick, however."

Mr. Van Allen raised a thin black eyebrow. "What's this? Are we doing a play?"

Lizzy nodded. "Yes, and there are still several roles we need to fill, if you and Mrs. Van Allen are interested. There is certainly no compulsion, however. I hope you will do just as you like."

"And Miss Crawford is to be Beatrice?" His dark eyes laughed at her. "She does love to act."

Mary smiled coldly.

"Oh, please do it, Uncle Fitz," Eleanor said. "It would be perfect."

"Perfect," Maggie was more subdued, but earnest.

Colonel Fitzwilliam looked to Mary.

She shrugged. "They are quite taken with the idea, but you must suit yourself. It is a matter of indifference to me."

Isabella sighed. "I suppose if Fitz will not do it, we will get another gentleman. Harry Hawksley could carry off the humor, but I doubt he could memorize a single couplet unless it was emblazoned on a prime bit of flesh."

Her mother gasped. "Isabella!"

"I meant a horse, Mother—what did you think I meant? Mr. Hawksley is obsessed with horse races."

Mary stifled a laugh and noticed Colonel Fitzwilliam's lip twitching.

"That is still an extremely vulgar phrase." Lady Matlock pressed two fingers to her temple. "You *must* watch your tongue, my dear."

Colonel Fitzwilliam raised a hand. "Fine. In the interest of pleasing my little sister—and paying off any debt I owe her now or in the future—I will play Benedick."

"Thank you, Fitz," she said.

He shook his head. "Take care—this is a serious deal you are making. Someday, ten years from now, I'm going to do something heinous, and you're going to want vengeance; and will you get it? No. You won't. Because I will remind you of this very moment."

"Rather Faustian of you," Mary murmured, "Dangling people's hopes in front of them to make life-altering bargains."

Colonel Fitzwilliam tilted his head to the side. "Any bargain is life-altering if you live long enough."

"Touché."

"Fitz," Isabella glared at him. "You said you'd never heard of Goethe! You didn't know how to say his name. Yet you and Miss Crawford know Faust well enough to *jest*?"

He laughed. "I may have pulled your leg a little to distract you. I've heard of him. He's famous, and so is his Faust."

"Oh—" Her curls quivered. "How dare you make fun of me! I declare *you* owe *me* the favor of playing Benedick."

"Perhaps I do." He half-bowed to Miss Crawford. "If you'll accept me as your partner, ma'am."

Mary was again taken aback by the appealing warmth in his eyes as he rose from his bow. Colonel Fitzwilliam was not precisely a handsome man, but there was something stupidly likeable about him. Unfortunately, he still disapproved of her; he was still a younger son. It did not matter what he looked like.

"The children want it so much," Mary said, "I don't see how I could say no."

Mr. Van Allen had been listening to this exchange with amusement. "Odd, generally you're very good at saying no."

"Would you like a part, Mr. Van Allen?" Isabella asked. "There are still several good roles—"

"No, no. Not for me. I prefer to watch, it's a better view." He met Mary's eyes boldly, but thankfully the conversation moved on.

Mary slipped away from the party at that end of the drawing room to a nook just around the corner. The room was an L shape, and this bit was surrounded by low cabinets and several shelves with interesting curios. It was dim, with less light from the windows and fire. There were only two chairs, and one was occupied by Harold.

"It's bedlam out there, isn't it?" he said. "I've hidden away."

"I might join you for a moment. Are you sure you don't want to participate? There are roles aplenty."

He stretched out his legs and rested his hands on his paunch. "Eh, it's not in my line. You've known me for five years; you know I don't put myself out if I don't need to."

"Five years? Take care, you'll make me feel dreadfully on the shelf."

He crossed his ankles, which were rather delicate compared to the bulk of the rest of him. "You're no more on the shelf than any of those young 'uns out there. You could've had Watts or DeCourcy, or even Van Allen last year—" He grimaced. "Er, I forgot about that scene the other night. I've a loose tongue, forgive me."

"It's nothing."

Lord Matlock looked uncomfortable. "He isn't being stupid, is he? Van Allen, I mean."

"No, of course not."

Lord Matlock looked dubious, but he only nodded and went back to the newspaper in his lap.

Mary eyed him. Yes, Harold would do nicely if he could be brought around to offer for her. A bit indolent, a bit of a gossip and gambler, but no idiot. She could not marry a stupid man, but an intelligent one that left her heart untouched?

Perfect.

{8}

LIZZY WAS GLAD TO TAKE A BREAK from the noisy business of planning the theatrical to greet Emma and Mr. Knightley.

They arrived about two hours after the Van Allens, but the temperature did not seem to have risen much from the morning. It was still icy cold, and the thick clouds promised either a freezing rain or more snow. The little snow that had fallen blew about like dust, building up in crevices and on the bare garden, but not sticking.

Lizzy again waited in the hall, though this time Darcy was with her. At her third shiver, he wrapped an arm around her, and she leaned her head against his shoulder. Thankfully the clouds held off while Mr. Knightley led Emma inside and two of the Pemberley footmen fetched their things.

Emma rubbed her gloved hands vigorously before holding one out to Lizzy. "How do you do, Mrs. Darcy? It has been so long."

Lizzy squeezed it in a friendly fashion. "What, are we back to honorifics? You must call me Lizzy like you used to, and you must give me permission to call you Emma, for I shall certainly forget and do so."

Emma smiled a little wider while the men greeted each other. "Very well, then. It smells of cider—I do hope there might be some in the near future."

"Yes, indeed! Apple cider is a winter tradition at my home, and Darcy has indulged me."

A silence fell rather abruptly after the first round of questions about travel and the weather. Mr. Darcy and Mr. Knightley were good friends, but they were unexpectedly stiff with one another.

Lizzy and Emma had written to each other once or twice since the spring, but it could not be denied they'd had a turbulent time in Highbury. They'd disagreed sharply about Harriet Smith, and then Lizzy's short engagement to Mr. Knightley had hurt Emma. That engagement had been a mistake Lizzy quickly shook off—but she hadn't been around Emma or Mr. Knightley much since then. Lizzy had supposed her own marriage to Mr. Darcy would have allayed all awkwardness, but perhaps she was wrong.

Lizzy clapped her hands. "We mustn't stand around here freezing. James will show you to your room. I'm sure you both want to freshen up. I'll have hot cider waiting for you in the drawing room, or mulled wine if you prefer."

Lizzy and Darcy tacitly waited for a few moments after Emma and Knightley went up the stairs.

"What is the matter?" Lizzy asked quietly. "Are you not happy to see your friend?"

"I am." Darcy became sadly tight-lipped when he was experiencing any strong emotion.

"You did not seem so."

"Nor did he."

Lizzy sighed. "I know it is a little awkward, but we must find a way past it. You have been good friends for a long while—ten years?—I'm sure you can weather this. Both of you are reasonable and mature men, and you are both happily married now." She started up the stairs and Darcy followed her.

"Still. You were engaged to him..."

"I was, but that can't be helped." Lizzy suddenly paused on the stairs, her hand on the smoothly oiled banister. "Do you have questions about that?"

He shook his head, but his brow was furrowed.

"Oh, my dear." Lizzy kissed his cheek; it was easy since she was a step above him. "You have no need to wonder. I never even *fancied* myself in love with him. He did not once kiss me... there was nothing. We were friends."

"I know. And I would not blame either of you if there had been more—" He shook his head. "No, I believe I feel sorry for him. How can I meet his eye knowing he almost married you, but then ended up with Miss Woodhouse? Mrs. Knightley, I mean. Can he be happy?"

Lizzy laughed, nearly bending over in her mirth. "Oh. That is not at *all* what I thought was going through your mind. Of course he can be happy! He is *far* happier with Emma, just as you are far happier with me. Ugh, men! They think whatever they have is best."

He squeezed her hand. "What I have *is* the best."

"Granted. Now, go up and invite Mr. Knightley to play billiards or to drink brandy in your study and clear the air. I will introduce Emma to the others."

Mr. Darcy did invite Knightley to the billiard room. He also poured an inch of brandy for each of them when they got there.

"Devilish cold," Darcy said. "Sorry you got caught in it. I hope Mrs. Knightley wasn't too disappointed."

"Emma? No, she is too excited to visit the Peak District to let a little cold bother her. She was bemoaning her lack of paints or pencil, so that she could capture the dramatic scenery and clouds we passed. She has not traveled much at all; she was very happy to come."

"I'm glad."

Mr. Knightley shot first and scattered the set of balls, sending them rolling in every direction. "We both appreciated the invitation to Pemberley."

"We are glad to have you."

"How are you and Mrs. Darcy?"

"Very well, thank you." It was one thing for Lizzy to tell him to clear the air. It was another to do so. Mr. Darcy took his turn. "I—er, I hope there's no unpleasantness—no awkwardness in being here."

He finally looked at Mr. Knightley and saw amusement in his friend's eyes. Knightley was in his late thirties, rather older than Darcy. Perhaps if Darcy had had an older brother, the relationship might have been like theirs.

"I hope there's no awkwardness as well," Knightley said. "In fact, I have only one question."

"Yes?" Darcy looked away to line up his shot and hide his face.

"Why didn't you *tell* me you were in love with Miss Bennet? I never would have proposed to her if I'd known."

Darcy could feel his own face turning red. "For that matter, you said nothing of your feelings for Miss Woodhouse."

"I did not know."

"Nor did I."

They faced each other for a moment, then Mr. Knightley clapped him on the shoulder. "We're a pair of fools then, aren't we?"

"I suppose we are." Darcy smirked. "However, you are the older and wiser one of our friendship; I can safely lay most of the fault at your doorstep."

Mr. Knightley scoffed, turning back to the table. "I take only half. If you were not so excessively stoic, I might have caught a hint. I'm surprised you didn't plant me a facer before you left Highbury."

"I wanted to, trust me."

"In retrospect, I can see it." He laughed. "To think of you grumbling under your breath and white-knuckling when you found out I was engaged to Elizabeth...! It makes me chuckle, but I promise I'll not mock you all week."

"Just the better part of it."

"Nonsense. I'm a gentleman. I'll limit myself to two days." He made another shot. "There must be something in these familial matches. Here's my brother and I, both wed to a Woodhouse lady. You and Bingley, both wed to Bennets. Sometimes things work out as they ought."

"That's terribly sentimental."

"We are married now. Sentiment is allowed. When you're my age—"

Darcy finally laughed. "Finish the game, Knightley, and we'll rejoin our better halves."

Colonel Fitzwilliam did not know quite what to think of Miss Crawford's behavior. As he watched the party that night, he could not help watching *her*.

Throughout dinner—slow-roasted duck and seasoned game hen, trout in a white sauce, braised winter vegetables in butter, and several jellies and sweetbreads—he couldn't help but listen to her, observe her.

She chatted with Emma Knightley, who had just arrived, and they seemed to good-naturedly recognize in each other a rival in strength of will and entitlement. She chatted with Harold. She laughed with Mr. Knightley.

She leaned toward Mr. Darcy to make several pithy observations.

She was so quick and dynamic and witty. She was hard to look away from, but that was the problem, wasn't it? Fitz was a little on his guard ever since the Sefton's ball. Mary Crawford had a reputation. Perhaps it was largely unearned—he'd thought so, at any rate, for Fitz did not like to believe the worst of anyone, and particularly not a lovely woman. However, it had been somewhat born out at that evening. Her young friend, Mrs. Van Allen, had clearly been upset and overwrought by her husband dangling after a noted Cyprian. Miss Crawford had done nothing to help her, and some that might make it worse.

Fitz was far from assuming Mary had flirted with Mr. Van Allen that night—though it *had* appeared that way. But even if she had not, when she sat back at the table, she had devoted herself to Harold and all but ignored her friend. It had not been kind.

She did not spend much time speaking to Mr. Van Allen tonight, as Fitz had half expected, but she hardly had a chance. She was not seated near him, and in the drawing room after dinner, he did not seek her out. As she interacted with first one gentleman and then another, Fitz felt his concern grow. She was part of a fast set, and sometimes ladies of that sort grew addicted to drama and attention. They did not necessarily go beyond the line, but they enjoyed stirring the pot. They liked gaining the admiration of unavailable men, provoking jealousy, or merely exploiting insecurities and instabilities in those around them.

Fitz did not want any pot-stirring at Pemberley. Darcy, for one, didn't deserve it. He was the best of good fellows, and he had had a trying year. There had been the rumors that followed Jane and Lizzy Bennet after their engagements. Not to mention the duel over Miss Fairfax when Darcy had taken a ricocheted bullet to the arm and been carted off to his club. That had caused more rumors.

Everything was dying down now, and hopefully this house party would be the end of it. But as Fitz watched Miss Crawford flirting with Harold and Mr. Knightley as they played whist—and she *was* flirting, there really was no other way to describe it—he didn't like it.

Her golden gown set off her figure and her complexion, and it caught and reflected the candlelight from every table.

He disliked the whole thing so much that he was unhappy by the time everyone gathered for tea before the party broke up for the night. Miss Crawford took her cup and saucer and moved away to make space around Lizzy for others to receive theirs; Fitz stepped aside with her.

"Enjoying your time at Pemberley, Miss Crawford?"

"Yes, indeed. It's a very homey scene, isn't it?" She gestured to Isabella and Georgiana sitting aside and talking, to Lizzy and Mrs. Gardiner near the fireplace, to Darcy and Knightley leaning against a side table and debating about something. Her eyes lingered on Mr. Van

Allen and Mr. Gardiner, who were playing chess in the corner. "Very... wholesome."

"That is an interesting adjective."

"You probably think I would not know wholesomeness if it was wrapped in ribbon and presented to me with a card, but I have a passing acquaintance with it."

This was so near what he had been thinking, he flushed. "Not at all. Iwas thinking that it is a far cry from my Christmases abroad. When we were quartered in Lisbon or another city for the winter, the balls were endless and not at all... wholesome."

"You need not tell me. My uncle hosted lavish house parties for his navy friends every year. There may be many a good *captain*, but there is not much admirable about the Admiralty."

"Too true, or so I've heard. I hope none of the taint of town or *ton* will encroach on Pemberley this year."

"Yes, you must hope—" She broke off and her jaw clenched. Her knuckles whitened where she gripped her dainty floral teacup. "Is that hint meant for me? How complimentary."

If she'd looked at all hurt or self-conscious, Fitz would have backed down.

Instead, her eyes glittered in a hard fashion, and her chin firmed. "I'm glad the Army of Occupation taught you to insult a woman with such an economy of words. Was that taught before or after conservation of ammunition?"

"I intended no insult, though perhaps a slight suggestion. Save your smiles for the unmarried men of our party. We don't need any drama beyond the children's theatrical." Fitz had not thought of it before, but the whole situation reminded him very much of house parties when he was a child. His mother and father had had a good relationship, but his mother had been hurt by his father's flirts. Fitz never found out, or cared to inquire, how far afield his late father had gone.

Miss Crawford raised her brows. "Oh, my. Was I too friendly with Mr. Darcy? Did I laugh at Mr. Knightley's joke at dinner? How brazen of me." She sipped her tea. "Perhaps you ought to tell Mrs. Darcy not to seat me next to any susceptible gentlemen in the future. I myself would have thought both Mr. Darcy and Mr. Knightley deeply committed to their wives, but I bow to your better knowledge."

Fitz grimaced. "You're trying to provoke me by attacking, but I am famously even-tempered."

"No, *I* am angry, and I do not very much care how you feel. Besides, I always prefer attack to retreat. Women in general are far too prone to retreat. They think it safer, perhaps, while in truth, an offensive strategy is usually best."

Fitz sighed. "Perhaps I should not have said anything—"

"Oh, do not retract now, I beg you. I cannot stand a man who will not own up to his true opinions."

They had both moved closer together. Lizzy's voice cut through their tension. "Miss Crawford? You promised to play for us tonight?"

They both realized that this had been repeated at least once before. They stepped apart at once. Miss Crawford gave him a bright, insincere smile. "Excuse me, sir."

She went to the head of the drawing room where Lizzy had instructed one of the footmen to bring out the harp that usually resided in the music room wrapped in cotton-wool.

Now it was uncovered, and it shone with touches of brass and gold in the firelight. Miss Crawford seated herself next to it on the narrow stool, moving the folds of her dress to lay nicely and not impede her.

She slid her left foot forward to brace her position as she put her fingers to the strings.

She fired off a stinging hail of notes as she began.

Fitz reclined on a nearby divan next to his brother Harold. Miss Crawford was an excellent harpist, but he suspected this song was supposed to be gentle and rippling. She all but glared at the floor as she played. Her fingers plucked the strings decisively, almost angrily. Instead of a cascade, it was a fusillade.

The harp being what it was, and her skill-level being high, even her ill-humor and aggression came out beautiful. The party sat quietly for the first song, as was customary.

Harold's eyes were half-shut by the time she went to the second song. She must have exorcised her ill-humor, for this song as different from the last. Harold raised one eye lazily. "She's quite good. This one is going to put me to sleep."

"I'm not going to carry you to bed."

Harold let his eyes shut. "You were having some sort of intent chat with the lady. Are you thinking of moving that direction? Good choice. I wouldn't mind having her around."

"That is *far* from my intention."

"You needn't cut up stiff. She's an heiress, good fortune, witty—might as well."

Fitz breathed slowly in and out his nose to calm himself. As a younger son, he received none of the land of Matlock Park, and only a small jointure from his mother, plus what he had from the Army. He had not saved as much as he perhaps could have. In short, he ought to marry a lady of fortune. In most respects, Miss Crawford was perfect, but Fitz had rather high standards. Lizzy, for instance, would have been perfect, if she hadn't been in love with Darcy and had only a tiny portion.

Fitz did not often give in to jealousy, but he'd had to subdue a passing regret as he got to know his cousin's wife. But Fitz was far happier for Darcy than he was melancholic for his own prospects. If he could've lifted a finger to change positions with Darcy, he would've worn lead gloves.

Harold snored slightly. Fitz jabbed him with an elbow to the ribs.

"Oi, none of that." Harold raised his eyes to half-mast with some difficulty. He yawned. "What were we talking about?"

"We weren't, but you were snoring."

"It was Miss Crawford."

"You're a bother."

He yawned again. "She could do better than you."

"I know. Why don't you marry her?"

Harold ignored this. "It might get her out of a sticky situation."

"Probably of her own making."

Harold frowned, hoisting himself to sit up a little straighter. "Rather insulting, aren't you?"

"You're rather concerned."

Harold shrugged. "Suit yourself."

Fitz watched the rest of her harp recital with his arms folded defensively over his chest.

{9}

MARY CRAWFORD WAS AT HER WITTIEST and best with the new gentlemen who arrived the following day. The house party was complete now that Mr. Holbrook and Mr. Hawksley had arrived.

They were quite different from one another, although they were apparently friends. Mr. Hawksley was short and round of body and face, with fair curly hair. He was handsome and jovial enough to figure as a very good-looking youth. Mr. Holbrook was taller and plainer, though his dark hair was thick, and his profile was good, despite his large forehead and nose.

Mary did not look to see how Colonel Fitzwilliam reacted to her friendliness to these two gentlemen. Let him judge her; she was still angry. The only gentleman she surreptitiously avoided was Mr. Van Allen. He continued making occasional comments that *she* knew to be inappropriate, but he had not done more.

When they all went into dinner that evening, Mary was placed between Mr. Knightley and Colonel Fitzwilliam.

On Mr. Knightley's right side was his wife, Emma, which was rather odd. Generally husbands and wives were seated apart from one another to allow them to engage in conversation with someone they did not see every day. Lizzy must have relaxed this rule in making up the seating arrangements.

As it was, Mr. Knightley was friendly, but he was more attentive to his wife than to Mary. This left her to converse with Colonel Fitzwilliam. If she'd thought he'd arranged to sit by her—to judge her or observe her or some such thing—she would have been excessively angry. As it was, his stiff and uncomfortable face showed that he had had nothing to do with it.

Mary found her ire dying down, and a malicious sort of amusement taking its place. Every dish that was served, she commented on to him. Every polite reply he made, she reacted as if he'd said something funny or clever. She asked him questions about his preferences, about his history, about his friends. She devoted herself to conversing with him, and she developed a crick in her neck from how often she leaned close to say something below the general hubbub.

Being a well-bred gentleman, he could not ignore her.

To talk was no punishment to Mary. She had been bred up in military circles and among the *haut ton.* She learned to dissemble when she could barely lisp, and to control conversations when she was barely out of leading strings. She punished Colonel Fitzwilliam with attention and conversation, and she felt vindication at each stiff response and even more so with each reluctant smile.

By the time the ladies left the table, while the men remained for their port, Mary was in a much better mood.

There were now fifteen adults in the house party, seven women and eight gentlemen. The ladies retired to one of the drawing rooms, the one which contained the harp Mary had played the previous evening. She had played it more roughly than the instrument deserved. It was truly a magnificent thing.

She found herself gravitating towards it now. She paused to pluck a few strings and admire the tone.

Lady Matlock, as a countess, was the highest-ranking lady of the party, and as such, Lizzy showed her a certain amount of deference, in addition to being the first lady led to the dining room, and so on. "Would you like music, ma'am?" Lizzy asked. "We could ask Miss Crawford to play again, or we could retire to the music room with the pianoforte. Or if you prefer, I can have the card tables set out in a trice."

Lady Matlock settled herself near the fire, which had just been stoked. Pemberley was a well-built, well-insulated house, but the creeping cold could not entirely be shut out.

"I have not seen dear Bertie all day," Lady Matlock said. "He was telling me how he would memorize Dogberry's monologue, and I promised him I would listen to his progress."

Mrs. Gardiner, Bertie's mother, smiled though she also looked apologetic. "That is very kind of you, but please don't feel you must cater to him! As I'm sure you know, boys of that temperament love a fresh audience and they are not afraid to ask for it. Repeatedly."

Lady Matlock had had sufficient time to recognize the gentle good sense and propriety of Mrs. Gardiner and had unbent remarkably. "Yes, I *do* know. Do not worry. I shall not let him plague me, but it has been a long time since I had a little boy to indulge. If Mrs. Darcy is amenable, let us bring the children in a for a few minutes. We will send them away again when the gentlemen come."

Mary resigned herself to another interlude with the four children. Eleanor immediately came to sit next to her at the harp.

"It has a *great* number of strings," Eleanor said. "I am learning the pianoforte, but I want to learn the trumpet!"

Mary smiled. "I have some sympathy with that wish. Sometimes it would be satisfying to make a merry blast on a horn."

"Yes! Like a captain, or a general!"

"I don't believe the officers generally sound the horn. Sadly it is one of the non-commissioned officers, little better than a private."

Eleanor wrinkled her nose. "I suppose so. Are you excited about the play? Beatrice is a wonderful role."

"I am. I read through her scenes today. I found another copy of *Much Ado about Nothing* in the library."

"Oh, excellent. I am glad you have started! You and Uncle Fitz will need to practice together very much to get them right."

"I suppose so. I will memorize on my own for now. Your Aunt Lizzy and Miss Georgiana have agreed to shorten and simplify several parts of the play; that should help."

"But you *like* Uncle Fitz, don't you? You will not mind practicing with him?"

Mary stroked the strings of the harp, then pressed her hand to silence their vibrations. "Not at all."

"You do *like* him, don't you?"

Did the child realize what her emphasis meant? Or was she just excited about her new favorite person?

"I'm not well acquainted with him," Mary said. "How is *your* practice going? The maid has several important scenes."

"It's fine. Maggie and I think Uncle Fitz is very handsome. Do you?"

If Eleanor had been ten years older, Mary would have suspected a clumsy trap. As it was, Mary only sighed. Children did get these fixations. Mary remembered being quite enthralled by one of Henry's tutors at the tender age of eleven. It was quite ridiculous. Of course, he'd kissed her when she was only thirteen... Mary had forgotten about that. She shook her head. At least Eleanor's small *tendre* for the Colonel would be safe. "Certainly, he's handsome, if you think so."

Eleanor smiled happily. She tentatively reached toward the harp. "May I touch it?"

Mary was on more solid ground here. "Are your hands very clean? You must never touch a fine instrument with dirty fingers."

Eleanor showed spread her fingers wide. "Yes, very clean."

"Good. Then you gently pluck the strings in a short motion. You are not trying to *move* them like the string of a bow and arrow, you are only making them sing."

Eleanor obediently plucked a few strings gently. "They are stiff. And so sharp!"

"Yes, they are metal, very strong. You build callouses if you play for very long."

Eleanor tried again, a little more firmly. "It sounds like water flowing." She looked at her hands. "I don't have callouses yet."

"It happens in weeks and months, not minutes."

"Thank you for showing me." Eleanor slid off the seat and went to whisper to her sister.

Georgiana shifted to the end of the settee to be near Mary. "That was kind of you to teach Eleanor about the harp. You are good with children."

"Good heavens. If I am, I am not aware of it. I don't understand children."

"Don't you remember being a child?"

"I'm not sure I do. Henry and I grew up quickly. But tell me—how are you enjoying your first Season? I have seen you here and there in town, but I have not heard how you like it."

Georgiana colored a little. "It is fine. Everyone is very... kind."

"Kind, I see. May I speak plainly to you, Miss Darcy?"

"Yes, please."

"You are a considerable heiress like myself, and that creates its own challenges. It is odious to complain about a blessing that many are denied, and yet a fortune is not without drawbacks. People flaunt, flatter, and fill your ears with whatever they think most likely to attach you. If you ever need a listening ear, I am happy to oblige."

Georgiana grew pale, her delicate features almost waxen in the candlelight. "You almost sound as if you knew—Lizzy did not *tell* you, did she?"

Mary drew back a little. She had meant to offer a little worldly wisdom to Miss Darcy, she had not meant to stumble upon a secret. "No, she has told me nothing! I spoke only from my own experience. I did not mean to distress you."

"Oh."

Mary couldn't deny that she was rabidly curious; she loved a good story, but perhaps Georgiana's story did not yet have a good ending.

"My brother's tutor kissed me when I was thirteen," Mary shared instead. "I thought I was in love with him, but he was nearly thirty. It was terribly inappropriate. I only say this so you know that *everyone* makes mistakes. I am the last person in the world to judge you."

"I did make a mistake with an old friend. At least—I *thought* he was a friend. He flattered me, like you said, but Wickham only wanted my inheritance. I nearly eloped with him, but Darcy found out. It is not generally known..."

"I will not tell anyone. What a near escape! I will drop the topic at once and only punctuate it by saying that you are well out of it, and perhaps you are more prepared for the difficulties of society than I thought. Forgive me for making assumptions."

"Oh, I am still quite happy to hear any advice you care to give. I am sadly ignorant of how to deal with... everything." There was a distraction as the gentlemen entered the drawing room. Georgiana's eyes followed them, but Mary was not sure whether it was Mr. Hawksley or Mr. Holbrook she was watching.

"Which gentleman has your attention, my dear? I cannot quite tell."

Georgiana's pale cheeks grew pink again. "Nobody."

"Ah, this is like Odysseus and the cyclops. Is it the tall dark nobody, or the short, fair nobody?"

Georgiana was surprised into a laugh. "I really shouldn't say."

"Why not? Let me tell you, gossiping with a friend about a favored gentleman is one of society's chief pleasures."

Georgiana smiled shyly. "I suppose it would not hurt to tell you that I enjoy dancing with Mr. Hawksley. He is one of the first acquaintances I made in London."

"No harm at all. And not bad taste."

The men were dispersing around the room as small knots of conversation were broken up and reformed to include them. Mr. Van Allen chose to stand by Emma, and Mr. Knightley stayed nearby, watchful.

Colonel Fitzwilliam sat down next to Georgiana. "Getting a harp lesson?" he asked.

"No, but Mary let Eleanor pluck the strings."

Just then, Eleanor rushed up to Colonel Fitzwilliam. "Uncle Fitz, there you are." She had taken a piece of kindling and stuck it in the sash around her dress like a sword.

"What's this?" the Colonel said. "Do I see a pirate or a highwayman before me? Am I accosted?"

"Not today," Eleanor said. "I must go to the nursery now that the gentlemen have arrived, but I wanted to tell you something."

She motioned for him to lean over, and he obligingly bent down. She cupped her hands around her mouth and whispered something to him.

Mary only caught a word or two over the noise of the room—something about Miss Crawford and handsome.

He smiled quizzically, looking from Eleanor to Mary. "Does she? Well, my thanks for passing on the good news. Now goodbye, Miss Eleanor, and goodnight."

Mary's mouth opened and shut. Had that dreadful little girl told the Colonel she thought he was handsome? Mary had only said so to make Eleanor happy. Mary was not embarrassed, but she was a little annoyed and perplexed. What was the child's game?

The children left and Colonel Fitzwilliam hesitated. Mary thought he might make a joke out of it to clear the air—he was that type—but instead he only nodded to them and walked away.

Mary turned back to Georgiana. "Men are strange and irritating. Would you like a game of backgammon? I spied a very fine board in the cabinet around the corner."

It would have been pleasant to play against Georgiana, but somehow she was called away and Alicia Van Allen became Mary's partner.

It was not ideal, but Mary made the best of it. Alicia had liked her perfectly well until the last few months, when she'd begun to suspect her husband's amorous attention was wandering.

Under cover of the hubbub of the room, as Alicia rolled the dice and moved her markers on the thin black triangles of the backgammon board, she began to question Mary.

"How, exactly, did you wrangle this invitation for us?"

"What?"

"I'm friends with Isabella Fitzwilliam, and I am unfortunately acquainted with you, but that does not explain anything. Van thinks I am stupid, but I knew his excuses for subterfuge. *You* wanted him here; I see it all now." She passed the dice to Mary.

Mary had rarely been at such a loss. Clearly Van had lied to his wife. "I did *not,* I assure you. Were you not excited to come? I thought you viewed it as a treat—"

"Do not treat me like a child!" Alicia realized her voice had risen, and she lowered it. She sniffed, holding out a petulant hand for the dice. "You think you are so sophisticated and better than me because you have been out for years, but that just makes you *old.*"

Mary laughed, more from annoyance than amusement. "Such an accusation makes you sound even younger. I am sorry that you have had a trying year, but it is not *my* doing—"

Alicia all but flung the two dice on the board. "It is entirely your doing. Van told me how you begged him to take you in when you returned to London. He may be—weak, but you are making him worse."

"If you cannot stop speaking such things, at least *lower* your voice." Mary moved her counters almost at random. "If you are so upset, why didn't you feign illness or some such thing? Insist that you remain in London. Even now, you could insist that you need to return."

"Why don't *you*?"

Mary had not yet found another friend to stay with. She could show up at her uncle's house, but it was not her first choice for a number of reasons. She really ought to stop dragging her feet. There was Mrs. Fraser or Lady Stornaway—she must write to one of them.

"Well?" demanded Alicia.

"I can't leave on the instant. Besides, there is more snow expected."

Alicia scoffed, but even she didn't seem to expect that Mary could depart Pemberley on the instant.

Fitz spent the rest of the evening with Darcy and the two young men who'd arrived most lately. He felt a little off-kilter, and he could only blame Miss Crawford. He was not quite sure what her dinner game had been about, but he knew it was at his expense.

He suspected she had capped it off by teasing him through the little girl—by having Eleanor tell him how handsome Miss Crawford thought he was.

Oh, well. If he was being punished, so be it.

It looked like *she* was being punished by Mrs. Van Allen.

Eleanor and Maggie snuggled into bed, enjoying the warmth of the warmed mattress. The air of the room was cold, but under the multiple blankets with two hot bricks below, they were quite snug. Eleanor could indistinctly hear the voices of the adults from the floor below.

She wriggled a little. "It is going so well. Miss Crawford and Uncle Fitz will have to practice the play together, and tonight, she agreed that he is very handsome. I told him so."

Maggie turned onto her side. "I don't know, Eleanor—that might not be the thing. We don't want to embarrass them."

"Mother says there is nothing shameful in liking your husband."

"No, but they are not married yet. Perhaps we ought to leave them alone. They will probably do fine without us."

Eleanor scoffed. "That is poor-spirited. I only forgive you because you are tired."

"With a little more time, they might end up together anyway."

"But now there are even more gentlemen to distract Miss Crawford! She needs our help."

"Very well, but don't do anything drastic."

Drastic, Eleanor felt sure, was a matter of opinion.

{10}

FITZ HELD THE HEAVY COLLECTED WORKS of Shakespeare in his hands and flipped through the play. The library at Pemberley was a large, shadowy affair when the clouds were as dark as they were this morning. In addition, most of the drapes had been pulled completely shut to add another layer of insulation against the cold glass. The one fireplace did not stand a chance of sending its heat and light around and between the shelves and stacks.

The result was a library straight out of a Gothic tragedy.

Fitz moved one of the drapes aside, and saw that fat, large snowflakes were drifting down. Already clumps were forming over trimmed rose bushes, and the front drive was pristine and white.

Another few hours of this, and it would be perfect to take the children outside to sled.

He twitched the drape back into place and took the tome he'd found back toward the fire. "There is far more here than I recall. This looks like it would take five *days* to recite, let alone five hours."

Darcy sat in one of the large, upholstered chairs that was adjacent to the fire. He had an almanac open on his lap, and one leg crossed over the other. "It is your own fault. You needn't have said yes."

"You may feel no pressure to please those around you, but we are not all so situated."

"Nonsense. I approved the idea of a theatrical, thus pleasing everyone around me except you."

"Now you're looking smug. You ought to play Don Pedro; he always seemed a smug, smirking fellow."

"I never smirk, and I can't play Don Pedro. Mr. Van Allen has agreed to do so."

"And Mr. Hawksley will be handsome, naïve Claudio? How appropriate."

While Fitz was studying his part in the library, Miss Crawford entered the breakfast room.

Lizzy did not have a set time for breakfast. She allowed her guests to come and choose from the set out as they pleased.

Unfortunately, this meant one could never quite know who would be in the room. Surely it was particularly bad luck that it was only Mr. Van Allen. His plate was empty, but for a stiff rind from a ham and a peach pit. He was sipping coffee, which Lizzy's servants supplied as well as tea. The smell of the coffee was quite appetizing, but Mary hesitated in the doorway.

He looked up and smiled. "What, afraid of me?"

She entered. She'd told Colonel Fitzwilliam the truth, she far preferred attack to retreat. "Nonsense. Don't be stupid."

She took a plate and deliberated over the offerings. The fuzzy peaches were ripe and cool, they must have been carefully stored to make it all the way to December. She took two of those, as well as a small serving of cooked oats. She drizzled a tiny circle of honey over it.

Mr. Van Allen watched her the whole time, leaning back in his chair. He was a very handsome man, probably around the same age as Mr. Knightley. That was where the similarities ended. He was arrogant, careless, and selfish. She sat across the table and one chair down from him.

"How is Alicia enjoying Pemberley?" Mary knew the answer, but it seemed wise to start the conversation with a reference to his wife.

"Very well. She and Isabella Fitzwilliam talked literature all evening. I'm glad my dear wife has someone else to bore with it for now."

"Alicia may not be a literary genius, but she is not boring."

"I thought it would be amusing to wed the beautiful blue-stocking, the unexpected diamond of the Season, the star... but it isn't. You ought to pity me, Mary. I'm having a dreadful time of it."

Mary looked toward the door, but no one was coming. There were over thirty people in the house, if you counted guests and servants. She must have terrible luck. She ate her food without answering him.

"There's not even any amusement to be had here," he complained. "Mrs. Knightley is a highly finished bit of nature, but her husband had as well be fastened to her side. Mrs. Darcy is pretty, if a bit slim for my taste. She seems like she would give as good as she got with a little flirtation, but she came damn near mocking me to my face last night. Very uncouth. I can see why people say he married beneath him."

"What a tragedy to be surrounded by happy marriages."

"It is. I suppose in another few years they will be more fun. I've caught them too soon. Then there's Mr. and Mrs. Gardiner. Who are they, pray? I've certainly never met them in town, and why did they bring their spawn with them?"

"They are Mrs. Darcy's aunt and uncle, and you'd do well to treat them respectfully. The children are her cousins."

"At least Mr. Gardiner plays a decent game of chess. *That* is what I am reduced to—I'm just another old married man playing *chess* at a house party."

"Perhaps among wholesome people, even you can't help but be improved."

"A fate worse than death." He shuddered. "If I am reduced to this after one day, I'll have country morals before the trip is done. Take pity on me, Mary."

"No." She used a knife to cut slices from her peach. "If it were up to me, you would not be here."

He grinned. "That was a tidy bit of work. I chatted with Mr. Darcy for ten minutes and he had his lady send around an invitation three days later."

"I imagine he has your measure by now. As do I. Alicia has my pity."

His face darkened. "She got what she wanted. *I'm* the one—"

The door of the breakfast room finally opened again, this time admitting Colonel Fitzwilliam holding a large book. He was not Mary's *first* choice of a third for this breakfast, but it was better than nothing.

He looked from Van Allen to her and back again.

"Good morning," Mary said. "I see you've found another copy of Shakespeare. It is funny how they seem to proliferate."

"Yes, quite."

"Perhaps today we might practice the first act of the play," Mary said. "Eleanor is quite insistent on it."

"Certainly, but it will have to be after I take the children out to enjoy the snow. They will probably not last very long, but I did promise to take them."

"Yes, you must keep your promise. Perhaps I will go with you. I could certainly do with a walk."

"How about you, Van?" Fitz asked the other man. "Care to brave the snow with the children? You might have some of your own before too long."

Mary easily interpreted the flash of annoyance and horror in Mr. Van Allen's eyes; Colonel Fitzwilliam smirked. "Don't look so frightened. They're not that bad. You should get some practice."

Mary at once forgave most of Colonel Fitzwilliam's offenses against her, purely for the pleasure of seeing him mock Mr. Van Allen.

Fitz had thought his teasing of Van Allen would insure he didn't participate in their outing, but he'd guessed wrong.

The man presented himself in the foyer of Pemberley, well-wrapped up in a great coat of elegant design. Mr. and Mrs. Gardiner were bundled up with scarves, hats, gloves, and riding boots to brave the snow, and they had made sure their children had on as many layers of protection as they could fit. Two pairs of small pattens had been found to strap over the girls' shoes.

The littlest boy, Pip, could barely see over the voluminous purple shawl that had been wrapped tightly around his neck and face, leaving only a small opening for his eyes.

Several others had decided to brave the snow as well. Mr. Holbrook and Mr. Hawksley were game for it, though they wore far less and seemed to think they would be fine with a coat and riding gloves. Miss Crawford had come, and Georgiana.

Fitz helped Georgiana wrap a woolen scarf around her neck.

She spoke, muffled. "I tried to get Isabella and Mrs. Van Allen to join us, but they wouldn't. Where do you plan to take the children?"

"Towards the lake. They can coast down the hill that leads down to it, for there are no trees there to get in the way."

One of Darcy's servants had uncovered two sleds in the attic, which the two young gentlemen good-naturedly shouldered as they left the warmth of the house and began their hike.

Miss Crawford was delighted with the white world that awaited them. "This is striking, I must say. A little sunshine would be welcome, but just now I can appreciate even the clouds. They cast such colorful shadows on the snow—lavender, violet, and blue! It is melancholy but arresting."

The snow was five or six inches deep already, and anywhere it drifted was rather deeper. Whatever melancholy silence there might have been was broken up by the children.

Bertie whooped when he reached the edge of the drive and began to shuffle through shin-deep snow. Eleanor tramped unevenly at first, getting the feel for her iron and wood pattens, and soon was tramping over the snow as well. She was not whooping, but there were some excited yells.

Mr. and Mrs. Gardiner supervised their children, but mostly they let them run up ahead.

"It is useless to stop them," Mr. Gardiner told his wife. "They are too excited, and besides, the exercise will keep them warm. Let them enjoy themselves."

From the house there was a gentle slope up to the top of a low hill, and from the top, they could see down toward the lake. This side of the hill was steep enough for sliding.

"The lake is frozen!" Bertie cried. "Oh, what I wouldn't give for some ice-skating shoes. I've seen the dandies skating in Hyde Park; it looks such fun."

"I doubt it is thick enough for that," Colonel Fitzwilliam told him. He made the children promise not to go on the ice, and the young men put down the sleds.

"We ought to try first," Bertie said, "to make sure it is safe for Maggie and Eleanor."

Mr. Hawksley grinned. "That's the ticket." The sled was easily long enough for several people, and Mr. Hawksley was nearly as eager as Bertie. They sat together on the sled, with the heavier Mr. Hawksley on the back, and he pushed them off.

It coasted down beautifully, gliding a straight path through the snow on its two runners. The lake was far enough away that there was plenty of time for them to slow before they reached the ice.

"This is great!" called Bertie. At the bottom, they clambered to their feet. "You should try."

Mr. Gardiner and Colonel Fitzwilliam helped Maggie and Eleanor get situated on the other sled and gave them a solid push. Eleanor whooped loudly and even Mary smiled to watch them. She felt a creeping fondness for the little girl.

Mary also listened in on a stilted conversation between Mr. Holbrook and Georgiana—good heavens, had *she* ever been that young and awkward?—and she was relieved when Mr. Holbrook took a turn to slide with Pip.

Georgiana rode with Maggie and Eleanor on the other, and the three of them just fit on the sled with Eleanor's knees tucked up high.

Mr. Van Allen came to stand next to Mary. His nose was red, and he stamped his feet. "Blasted cold. I could be snug in a parlor in London right now."

"I wish you were."

"What and deprive Alicia of this outing? I think it was very thoughtful of me."

Mary shook her head. He *did* think it; he was too self-centered to realize that chasing a woman who was not his wife fully negated any kindness in bringing Alicia to Pemberley.

"You look cold." His hand slid around her hip, as he put his arm around her.

Mary jerked away from him. "I am not."

Unfortunately, her step took her to a part of the snow that had been trampled and slicked down by the sledders. Her riding boots slid out from under her, and she slammed onto her back. Her momentum had her sliding and then rolling halfway down the hill before she had understood what happened.

She was jarred, disoriented, and very cold.

"Miss Crawford! Oh, Miss Crawford!" She heard several of the party calling out to her.

"Ugh." She sat up and put a hand to her head. "I'm fine."

Her bonnet had been knocked back, and her hair must be a sight. She slid the bonnet back into place, though she could feel that the ribbons had knotted themselves under her chin. She would pick the knot later.

The cold and wet seeped through her pelisse and her skirt, and she must have scraped a fair bit of snow into her boots, for her stockings were soaked.

She tried to push herself up, but being on an incline did not help.

Colonel Fitzwilliam had been dragging one of the sleds back to the top, and he trotted over. "That was quite a tumble. Did you hit your head?"

"No, I don't think so. If you'll just assist me..."

He counterbalanced her as she got to her feet, and he steadied her as she planted each foot firmly in some of the uncrushed snow.

Eleanor was right behind him. "Are you hurt, Miss Crawford? Oh, please say you are not."

"I am not, thank you. Probably I shall have a few bruises, but I am only shaken."

Mr. Van Allen had descended from the top. "I say, Mary, that was a sight."

She gave him a hard stare. "I'm sure it was."

Mr. Van Allen held out a hand. "Allow me—"

But instead of taking Mary's hand, Eleanor shoved the rope of the sled into Mr. Van Allen's hands. "Yes, sir, thank you," she said. "I cannot pull it up by myself."

His face was comically annoyed.

Colonel Fitzwilliam wrapped Mary's hand around his arm and assisted her to climb back to the top of the hill.

Mr. Holbrook and Mr. Hawksley were just behind them, and the Gardiners waited at the top. Mary had to repeat her assurances to all that she was not hurt. She added, "That being said, if you will not think me a poor creature, I shall return to the house." Her toes were already quite numb.

"Yes, perhaps we all should," Colonel Fitzwilliam said. "It is very cold."

"Oh, not yet," begged Bertie. "Please, sir! Just a few more slides."

Eleanor agreed. "Yes, but *you* should go back, Uncle Fitz. You can make sure Miss Crawford is well. She looks very pale."

"I can see the house from here," Mary said. "I shall be fine."

"No, no—an escort for certain," Mrs. Gardiner agreed. "I should hate for you to slip and fall again."

Colonel Fitzwilliam looked conflicted. "You should not go alone, certainly. I had better stay with the children since I sponsored this outing—"

"No, no," Eleanor said. "Mama and Papa are here, and Mr. Hawksley and Mr. Holbrook are good at guiding the sleds! We shall be fine."

"We don't mind," said Mr. Hawksley. "I'm a bit keen to go again myself."

The only other gentleman with them was Mr. Van Allen, but Mary wasn't going to suggest him as a companion. "Very well, thank you all," Mary said. "We shall see you shortly."

Mary glared at Mr. Van Allen when he looked as if he might accompany them. She was annoyed with his flirtation, with his badly timed and public overtures, and with his selfish interest in herself.

Mr. Van Allen ignored her glare. "I'll go back as well—"

Before Mary could say anything, Eleanor spoke up. "We'll need your help to carry the sleds back."

"My dear girl—"

"No, she's right," Mary agreed. "Miss Darcy and Mrs. Gardiner and the children might need support on the way back. And who will pull the sleds?"

She turned with Colonel Fitzwilliam and they slowly made their way down the gentle slope toward the house, leaving an annoyed and stymied man behind.

The well-scythed lawn was covered with an immaculate blanket of snow, broken only by a few ornamental trees and their footsteps in a variegated path of purple and gray slush.

"I hope you won't find yourself stiff or pained tomorrow," he said. "I ought to have had you stand further from the edge. It could have been Mrs. Gardiner instead of yourself, and I fear she wouldn't have picked herself up so easily."

"It is not your fault. I'm sure it was a ridiculous sight; I know I flailed spectacularly."

He smiled. "Perhaps a bit, but I would never laugh at a lady."

"I shall laugh for the both of us. It is always better to laugh at oneself first, it inoculates one against ridicule."

"If so, I might start laughing at myself now about this theatrical. I will need an early start for the amount of ridicule I shall receive. I had forgotten how long it is!"

"Yes, it is rather long. Isabella will have to content herself with the players using the script as we go. A dramatic recitation of sorts, rather than a pure performance."

"That would help." He clutched her arm a little tighter when one of her feet slid a few inches.

"Thank you."

"Of course." He cleared his throat. "Am I—er—forgiven for the other day?"

Mary had almost forgotten about that. "Let's not canvas it again. I'll only grow angry once more, and I'm feeling charitable at the moment."

"Fair enough, Miss Crawford."

{11}

EMMA WOKE WHEN MR. KNIGHTLEY returned to their room. She yawned and stretched. "Is it very late? With this light, I cannot tell."

"Extremely late," he said, bending down to kiss her head. "I've come to make sure you're still alive."

She yawned again. "I'm a spoiled heiress, you know, who doesn't apply herself to anything. I can't be expected to wake early on holiday."

Mr. Knightley rolled his eyes. She was in the habit of teasing him with criticisms he may or may not have leveled at her in the past. She frequently made them up and almost always exaggerated them. "Yes, you are, my dear Emma, but even you usually get up before two in the afternoon."

"Good heavens." Emma sat up abruptly. "Is it really?"

"I was joking about your survival, but I did want to make sure you weren't getting sick." He put the back of his hand against her forehead, frowning. "You don't feel feverish to me. I hope the cold journey didn't leave you indisposed. Were you very tired yesterday evening? You didn't tell me."

"I was tired, but only from the carriage." Emma pushed her feet in the warm slippers that were tucked under the edge of the four-poster bed. She took up her dressing gown which was laid across a chair by the fire and shrugged it on. "My back aches a little, but I daresay that is from lying in bed too long. If my thoughtful husband felt like rubbing my shoulders for a moment..."

He turned her around, and Emma went almost limp as he rubbed her back. This was one of the best things about being married. Emma had been affectionate with her sister and her governess, Mrs. Weston, and she had not realized how much she missed physical affection until she married.

Her back unknotted, and her muscles relaxed as his thumbs rubbed circles over her shoulder blades. Her eyes were almost shut again when he pressed his lips against the side of her neck, inhaling deeply. "I love you, Emma."

He pressed another kiss just below her ear. His hands slid around her waist.

"Is Lizzy waiting for us?" she asked.

"It's already two, she could wait a bit longer."

Emma turned in his arms. "She certainly could. We'll blame it on me."

He had that certain look of wonder on his face that overcame him at times. He still seemed to be amazed that she was his wife, that they had this relationship. Emma caressed his cheek. "Did you lock the door?"

He turned back and flipped the key in the lock.

They didn't join the others until nearly three.

Mr. Van Allen was cold and stiff by the time he trudged back to the house. He was indeed given one of the sleds to carry on his shoulder.

He was a strong man, and it did not weigh him down, but it was annoying. Mr. Holbrook offered his arm to Miss Darcy, and Mr. Hawksley held the hands of the two little girls. Mr. Gardiner escorted his wife, and that left him and the older boy to handle the sleds.

He'd been relegated to footman status.

It was snowing again by the time they got back to the house, and Van's ears and nose were burning. Stupid weather.

To top it off, when he arrived back in the drawing room after his valet helped him change out of wet trousers, the Knightleys were there. They were so in love it was inappropriate. It was in the way she moved, and the way he smiled at her. It was just disgusting. Married people should not act like that, and was *everyone* in this benighted house having a better time than he?

Van found it annoying to be married. It had seemed a great lark at the time, and Alicia was a considerable heiress. It was a classic, time-honored story, and he had been willing to play the part of the reformed rake who fell for the beautiful debutante.

But it had never been more than a role, and he was tired of it now. For him, the thrill was in the illicit, and there was nothing illicit about marriage.

He cast himself on one of the divans near the fire—he was still cold—and looked about for entertainment. His wife was sitting nearby with Isabella. They were discussing the theatrical again, and she turned her head away when he made eye contact.

Alicia was tiresome.

Harold Fitzwilliam was dozing with a half open book resting on his protruding waist.

Mr. and Mrs. Knightley were talking to their hosts, and they made an insipid foursome of married bliss. The two young men—who didn't even know to appreciate their singleness!—had just begun a game of chess. Miss Darcy sat nearby with a piece of sewing and was partially watching the game.

It was sedate, calm, and *boring.* If he was trapped like this much longer he might end up doing himself an injury. Or reading a book.

After a while, he realized that Mary and Colonel Fitzwilliam must not be coming. They had returned to the house before the rest of the expedition, and they had had plenty of time to change and rejoin the others.

Mary Crawford was the only interesting woman in the house. He'd enjoyed flirting with her periodically through the years... why hadn't he asked *her* to marry him? Marriage might still ruin the excitement that existed between them, but at least she would not be so clingy and emotional as Alicia.

He rose with a grunt and went to investigate.

Pemberley was a large house. There were three floors and two wings, full of luxurious family rooms, fine guest rooms, colorful galleries, echoing drawing rooms, and cozy nooks and crannies.

Van suspected he'd find the errant couple in one of these nooks, perhaps between the stacks in the library, or tucked near the fire in the abandoned breakfast room, but he did not. Van didn't suppose Mary was much tempted by a plain-looking younger son like Colonel Fitzwilliam, but Van being who he was, he couldn't imagine the colonel wasn't like himself. It wasn't until Van heard raised voices from the ballroom that he found them. The door to the ballroom was half open, as the rug had gotten folded and caught.

He kicked the rug flat with his boot and entered. The ballroom was empty of furniture except for several tables and sofas under cloth against the far wall. Despite its large windows and the French doors that led to a balcony, the ballroom was rather dim. The broad floor was polished and smooth, and the echoing space went up to a high ceiling broken only by an unlit chandelier. All the panes of glass in the tall windows showed a snowy, frigid afternoon. The balcony was covered with snow, and the railing held an icy arch as well.

Colonel Fitzwilliam and Mary stood near the small platform for the musicians, the one soon to be used as a stage.

"I asked you not to bring it up again," Mary had just said. She rolled the script angrily in her hands. "To reverse the clichéd insult, you must be *less* intelligent than you look."

Colonel Fitzwilliam's hands were clasped behind his back, and his shoulders were stiff. Neither of them noticed Van in the doorway. "You *fell* earlier, Miss Crawford. I was attempting to express concern and make sure nothing untoward happened."

"By insinuating that I was flirting with Mr. Van Allen? You cannot stop yourself, can you?"

"My comment did *not* insinuate that. Perhaps your own conscience added the implication."

She paused and Van laughed. They both turned to look at him. Both faces, in their way, hostile.

"What are you doing here, Van?" Mary's use of his nickname was not lost on any of them. She compressed her lips. "Never mind. I shall have to practice later." She tossed her sheaf of paper down onto the platform and strode across the echoing floor.

"What have I interrupted?" Van said. "Is it possible, sir, you suspect Miss Crawford and I of a *flirtation*? What a shocking accusation." He said it in such a way as to confirm all the colonel's suspicions.

Mary slipped by him toward the door.

"Leave me alone." Her words were quietly spoken, for him alone.

He smiled. "Why? When he already thinks the worst of you?"

Van followed her out into the hall and paused. The two little Gardiner girls stood there, on their way to the nursery.

They studied each other. Van didn't like children; yet another reason he should not have got married. He needed an heir, obviously, but these small people with their clear gaze and unknown agenda almost made him ready to resign his estate to his fat cousin Barnard.

Mary passed by them toward the drawing room; Van backed away from them.

A book it was.

Fitz retired to the library, though not for a book. He poured himself a finger of Darcy's scotch. Darcy wouldn't mind, and Fitz could use a stiff drink. He truly hadn't insulted Miss Crawford again; she was merely—perhaps justifiably—quick to take insult and very defensive.

That didn't give conclusive evidence she *was* or *wasn't* involved with Van Allen, but Fitz had no plans to confront her about it. Frankly, as long as no mischief was started here at Pemberley, he did not care.

He didn't care at all.

It was Georgiana who broke his reverie some half an hour later.

"Uncle Fitz, I did not know you were in here." He was her cousin, not her uncle, but as one of her guardians, the nickname had stuck.

"Yes, I am." He raised a glass to her. "Being terribly unsociable."

"That is not like you." She sat down gently in the chair across from him. No log had been added to the library fire since morning, so it was little more than coals now. "Is everything well?"

He shook himself. "I should be asking *you* that. Your first house party! How are you liking it?"

"I am thankful that Darcy married Lizzy, and I do not have to be the hostess."

He laughed. "Yes, that worked out well. You'll have your own place eventually, but you have time to grow into it."

"I hope I won't *grow* at all, I'm already too tall!"

"Nonsense."

"I'm taller than Mr. Hawksley." Her cheeks turned red. "And—and several other gentlemen I've met this year."

Fitz sat up a little straighter from where he had slumped back. "Oh. Mr. Hawksley?"

He'd not thought—well, he had hoped that Mr. Holbrook was the one that grabbed her attention. Mr. Hawksley had just been invited for propriety and numbers.

Georgiana shook her head. "Don't tease me."

"I won't. It's just... he's not... never mind." Fitz had never been more thankful that Darcy married. Lizzy could have these conversations with Georgiana. "How goes the planning for the theatrical? I hope Isabella will consent to our carrying a script, for I shall need it."

"She is rather idealistic."

"*My sister,* idealistic? You jest."

Georgiana laughed. "Will you help me to lay out a drop-cloth on the stage? Darcy had a footman set up several boards, so I have a backdrop to paint now. It needs to be whitewashed before I can begin."

"I suppose I could help with that, but I must change first. Do you suppose the butler has a smock I can borrow?"

Fitz did end up with a smock, though where it was unearthed from, he did not know. No whitewash was to be found—"It's more of a spring activity," he explained to Georgiana—but a slightly dry cake of olive brown had been found and mixed to make a color she approved of.

"This brown will work just as well," she said, as Fitz used a wide brush to apply paint to the wood that had been put across the back of the stage. "Isabella and I decided that so much of the play takes place in the courtyards and gardens around Messina, that a garden scene would be appropriate. To this dark background, I can add bushes, flowers, and an arbor. Perhaps I'll try the vanishing perspective and imply paths."

"I'm glad you're enjoying yourself."

"Yes, thank you for helping! This part is the hardest."

"On the contrary," he slapped another brushful of paint at the wood, "this is easy. Don't ask me to paint any flowers."

"I meant physically this is the hardest part. The wood wants to soak up the paint, and it is too high for me to comfortably cover the whole thing. Thank you."

"You're welcome. I suppose we must let it dry after this?"

"Yes. I'll collect my paints from the school room, but probably I will not be able to begin until tomorrow."

She left to do so and came back as he was in the middle of the next coat. She left her paint things in a neat pile on the worn linen sheet beneath their feet. "I told Lizzy I would join them in the music room, but I feel guilty leaving you alone to work."

"Never fear," Fitz said. "I'm perfectly fine."

When the door opened soon after, he thought it was her again.

He didn't step down from the stool he was using to reach the top of the boards, but he looked over his shoulder. "Georgiana—oh, Miss Crawford?"

"Yes. I didn't realize—I just came to collect my script." She fetched her papers, which had been put to one side when he and Georgiana rearranged. "Excuse me."

But when she went back to the door of the ballroom, he heard her twist, pull, and even jerk at the door. She said something under her breath.

Fitz finished the last of the paint and set the brush down across the pail of murky brown. "Something wrong?"

"The door seems to be locked."

He frowned. "I don't see how it could be. You just entered."

"Yes, I know." She tried the door again. "Yet it will not open."

Fitz used the linen towel to rub his hands free of brown paint before joining her. "Darcy's servants would usually handle a door that sticks before it gets this bad, but perhaps the cold and moisture..." He tried the door several times, even giving it a smart thump with his boot. "It does seem to be locked, but that's ridiculous."

She looked at him. "Yes. Also, you have paint on your forehead."

Fitz stared at her, then laughed. "Do I? Excuse me." He went back to the stage and attempted to rub it off. Probably he just made it worse, based on the twist to her lips.

"What next?" she asked.

Fitz worked on the door a bit longer. "A very strange thing. Georgiana did mention to Mrs. Gardiner that she didn't want the children to come in here with the wet paint. Perhaps Mrs. Gardiner locked the door to be safe?"

"Without checking whether anyone was in here?"

It did seem odd, but he did not have another explanation. "I'm sure someone will realize you're missing and come to check on you." He immediately pictured Van Allen, but he pressed the uncharitable thought away.

"No, they won't. I took leave to lie down before dinner. I came in here to retrieve this before going to my room." She waved the script.

"Oh. They may miss me, then."

Her forehead furrowed. "You absented yourself most of the afternoon. As Darcy's cousin, you can do as you please at Pemberley without explanation."

"That is so."

Mary shifted her weight and stared at the offending door. Her head ached, her muscles quivered, and several bruises on her shoulders and backside smarted. She only wanted to lie down on the comfortable bed in her room, perhaps curl up under the soft wool blankets, and close her eyes.

Her nose was filled with the smell of paint and a little of Colonel Fitzwilliam, as she and he both crowded near the door. It was perfectly silent in the room, except for the faint ticking of a clock. The snow outside seemed to muffle all outdoor noises.

Very faint laughter came from the drawing room.

"Perhaps you could yell?" asked Miss Crawford.

"A fine figure I should cut."

"Looking a little ridiculous is a small price to pay for escape."

"If we wait a little longer—"

Mary sagged at the idea; her bruises nagged at her.

"Oh, you should sit. Are you feeling badly?"

"I have the headache and I am—" bruised, aching, frustrated, "tired."

He went across to the far wall where there were several items of furniture in Holland covers. He flicked one of the cloths up off a sofa, and it seemed to hang in the air for a moment, a billowing cloud in the dim light from outside. A chaise lounge was uncovered, and Colonel Fitzwilliam bowed. "At your service."

Mary was too tired to cavil. "Yes, I don't mind if I do." She picked up the cloth, rolled it into a serviceable pillow, and leaned back against the lounge with the cloth behind her head. Her feet were still on the floor, but she was half-reclined. "You could still yell for help."

He looked at her for a moment, something warm in his face. "Yes, I could."

Mary closed her eyes as he went back to the door.

"Hey! Hey there!" He knocked loudly on the door to punctuate his words. His voice was authoritative when raised. He was so affable and friendly (when he was not insulting her), that sometimes she forgot he had been a colonel. She imagined most officers learned to raise their voice to good effect.

In this case, he was not successful. After several tries—and his loud voice did nothing for Mary's headache—she relented. "You may as well wait. Those in the drawing room cannot hear you, and clearly there is no one in this part of the house at present."

In this she was wrong.

Eleanor, who had been told by her mother to leave the ballroom alone while the paint dried, had done a slight bit of investigating. On finding Uncle Fitz and Miss Crawford alone in the ballroom, she had had a rather good idea. It seemed to her that Mr. Van Allen or Mr. Knightley or *someone* was always interrupting promising moments between her new favorite couple. Perhaps they needed some time to have the *moment* her mother spoke of.

It was the work of an instant to shut the door and turn the key that lived unused in the lock above the doorknob. She set down the plain copper key on a funny bench in the hall, only a few feet from the door.

She paused there for a while, listening. She could hear their voices but not what they said. At least they were talking; that was good. Miss Crawford had a lovely voice.

Eleanor was tripping away happily when Colonel Fitzwilliam began to knock at the door. This gave her some pause, but Eleanor was not a child to second guess herself. Someone would be along soon enough, or she would come back herself in less than an hour. It was really quite difficult for two people to fall in love, for as her mother said, polite society "afforded very little opportunity for private conversation."

When Eleanor passed a footman going the other direction, with a confused look on his face, Eleanor felt it was too soon. She reassured him. "No, no, it's only Colonel Fitzwilliam and Miss Crawford practicing the play. They don't wish to be disturbed just yet!"

As the knocking also stopped, he seemed to take her word for it. "Ah, yes, miss. Very good."

Mary opened her eyes to see Colonel Fitzwilliam uncovering another chaise lounge. The Holland cover cast up a cloud of fine dust. Mary sneezed twice.

"Apologies," Colonel Fitzwilliam said. His own nose was twitching a bit. He rolled the cloth up and sat on his own piece of furniture. "Dashed odd circumstance."

"I suppose you are more to be pitied than me. This must lacerate your high standards of propriety." She closed her eyes again. Her back still hurt. She moved her makeshift pillow to the end of the lounge and used a finger to pull her slippers off. She brought her feet up, curled on her side, and tucked her hands under the rough cloth. It was rather cold in here, but at least she was not aching so much now. She tucked her feet inside her skirt like a blanket.

She heard him sigh. "I'm not obsessed with propriety, ma'am."

"You've played the part remarkably well."

"I don't care about manners; I care about... people."

It was a good answer, she admitted to herself. She didn't tell him that.

When Miss Crawford was silent for a long while, Fitz assumed she was still angry with him. It wasn't until he sat up and leaned forward, bringing her back into view, that he realized she had fallen asleep.

She looked cold, curled in on herself, and small. She was such a strong-willed, vibrant person, it was easy to forget that she was not larger than life. Her shawl was bunched up around her neck and shoulders. A darkening bruise peeked from beneath her peach sleeve. Her brow was still a little furrowed.

He wanted to sit next to her and spread her shawl over her properly. He wanted to undo her hair and rub her scalp until her headache was gone and her face relaxed. He wanted...

Fitz turned away, surprised at the strength and direction of his own wishes. He removed the Holland cover from one of the tables, shook it out quietly, and draped it over her. It reached from her arched foot to her chin, offering at least one layer of protection.

{12}

ELEANOR WAS NOT A FORGETFUL sort of a child, and she certainly did not forget what she had done. When she judged that an appropriate amount of time had elapsed—based partially on the clock and partially on the very good seed cake that was delivered to the schoolroom—she returned to the ballroom.

Quiet as a mouse, she put the key back in the lock and turned it. She pressed her ear to the door, but she did not hear anything. That was odd, but she also had a strong sense of self-preservation and she resisted the urge to open the door and check if they were really in there. Her motives were extremely good, but she knew she would get in trouble if found out.

As quietly as she'd come, she slipped back up the stairs to the school room on the second floor. Perhaps there would be more seed cake if Bertie and Pip had not gorged themselves in her absence.

Thus when Fitz tried the door again, in a fit of frustration at being trapped in a cold ballroom with nothing to do but add a layer of paint to Georgiana's backdrop and stew in his own feelings...the door opened.

He stumbled a half step when it gave way, as he'd twisted the handle rather viciously.

"What the *deuce*?" He stepped into the hall that led down this wing of the house. There was no one in sight. The brass key rested in the outer lock of the door, as innocent as you please.

He turned the key several times. He opened and shut the door. It did not stick. The floral carpet runner in the hallway did roll up slightly, but that would keep the door *open* not shut. Though perhaps if a child had kicked it up while they were inside...

"Miss Crawford?" he said. "Miss Crawford—we're free to leave now."

She must be very deeply asleep, for she didn't respond. He finally resorted to touching her shoulder, giving her a gentle shake. "Miss Crawford?"

She roused with a jerk. One arm came in front of her chest defensively, the other pushed her to a sitting position. Her feet hit the floor with a slap.

He backed off a step. "It's just me—it's Colonel Fitzwilliam. You fell asleep in the ballroom, but the door is open now."

Between one blink and the next, she'd put herself back together. Her chin rose, her feet slipped back into her shoes. "Good." Her voice was a little throaty and hoarse. She cleared her throat. "Did we find out what mischief was at work?"

"I am at a loss. I tried the door again and it opened easy as you please."

She rose to her feet, wincing at hidden bruises. "That is strange, but we are not far from Scotland, perhaps it was one of the elusive brownies of folklore. We must listen for clangs and bumps in the night to confirm."

"I did notice that the carpet rolled up, just here," he showed her, "but I cannot see that it would have kept the door firmly shut."

"Perhaps it was Mrs. Gardiner, like you suspected."

"Perhaps." Fitz pocketed the key. "I'll just put this somewhere safe. In the meantime, you may as well go up to your room and rest, Miss Crawford. Apparently we were not missed for an errant hour, so you may as well go while you can."

"Yes, I shall. Please give my excuses to Mrs. Darcy for this evening. I don't believe I will come down for dinner."

"Certainly. I'm sure she'll have something sent up to you. Please—" He hesitated. "You probably don't wish for advice from me at present, but recollect I've been in the army. Perhaps you should ask your maid to stay nearby tonight. You might have hit your head when you fell, even though you didn't lose consciousness. Sometimes it happens that way. Your lethargy worries me."

Miss Crawford frowned. "My sleepiness has normal causes. I have not slept well the past several weeks. However, I will take your advice under recommendation."

She retreated up the stairs and Fitz went to the drawing room.

When he entered, he expected at least a few questions; where have you been, or what kept you?

Instead, the tranquil scene in the drawing room barely rippled at his entrance. There was a game of whist going, the two young men were now playing piquet, and his brother Harold was fast asleep. Darcy was writing a letter, and Mrs. Knightley was reading a book, though she looked as if she too might fall asleep.

Only Georgiana really noted his arrival. "Thank you again for painting the boards."

"Certainly." He dropped into a chair. Let that be a lesson in humility to him. "I say, Darcy, I got stuck in the ballroom just now, or else someone locked it. I couldn't get the door open at all, kicked it even."

Darcy paused his letter writing, tipping the pen so no ink would drip on the paper. "Oh? That's strange. How did you get out?"

"I tried again, and it just opened." Fitz didn't see fit to mention that Miss Crawford had been stuck in there with him. The point was to make sure it did not happen again. He explained a little what had happened. "Do you think someone might have locked it?"

Lizzy looked over from her cards. "I doubt it, but I'll make sure my aunt and the servants know not to lock any rooms! That's very strange. I'll have the carpet attended to also."

That was really all there was to be said, so Fitz took up a newspaper. He was still not fit to deal with his own feelings as yet.

Isabella Fitzwilliam organized the first official read-through of the play that evening after dinner. She and Georgiana had been busy finding and making extracts of the pertinent scenes for each player.

Those with the most lines in any scene were granted permission to hold one of the three official copies of *Much Ado About Nothing* that they had found in the library. These could be passed around as needed. Those with smaller roles had been given just their lines with a few cues as to the scene and the exchange.

The children were present, since they had lines, and most of the adults as well. Harold had gone around the corner to the reading nook with Mr. Darcy, since neither of them were part of it.

Logs had been added to the fire, and multiple lamps brought in so that no one would have to squint uncomfortably at the small words. Georgiana sat between Eleanor and Pip, who was the youngest, and might need help reading his lines. The room was full of a warm glow, and Isabella felt the glow all the way to her toes. She was quite in her element as mistress of the room, and she enjoyed bossing her elders about.

"Now, even though we are merely reading through the script, we can add *feeling.* Without feeling, a play is just words. Miss Crawford is tired this evening, so I will read Beatrice during her scenes, and Alicia—Mrs. Van Allen, I mean—will read as Hero."

Isabella looked at the neat list of names that Georgiana had copied out for her, the cast list. "It could not be arranged with perfect consanguinity of actors to roles—"

Her brother Fitz raised a hand. "I'm not sure you are using that word correctly."

"Yes, consanguinity—as in, similarity."

"It means to be a blood relation, to have a common ancestor, like you and I."

"Don't interrupt, Fitz. The *point* is that we cannot have actors that all match their parts—mostly because we have more women than men who are willing to participate. For instance, Mrs. Knightley agreed to be Leonato, the rich landowner and father of Hero." Isabella had been surprised that the beautiful and poised Mrs. Knightley had actually *wanted* that part.

"Of course," Emma replied. "He is at the center of everything, and I do like that, I admit. We have only to make me the *mother* of Hero instead of the father, and I can still be a rich landowner. Anywhere that Leonato is referred to as *he,* we can simply change to she."

"I agree." Isabella continued, "To set the scene, a messenger has come from Don Pedro to tell of the end of the battle. Señor Leonato, Hero, and Beatrice hear his message."

Mr. Holbrook was the messenger and several other incidental roles. "Does that mean I have the first line of the play? I thought this was a small role." He looked betrayed.

"It *is,*" Isabella assured him. "And you don't, Emma—I mean, Mrs. Knightley, has the first line of the play. You just have to be in the first scene as the messenger."

Mr. Holbrook sighed.

Emma began with relish. "I learn in this letter that Don Pedro of Aragon comes this night to Messina."

Mr. Holbrook read, "He is very near by this: he was not three leagues off when I left him."

"How many gentlemen have you lost in this action?"

Mr. Holbrook read, "But few of any sort, and none of name."

Isabella could not let this continue. "Mr. Holbrook, you really must inject *some* feeling into your voice. You sound as if you are reciting a recipe."

Her mother frowned her down. "Isabella, my dear, it is not your place to critique Mr. Holbrook."

"But yes, it is. I am the director! He does not mind, I'm sure."

"No, no," he assured Lady Matlock. "I did agree to help."

"Try again," Isabella said.

They got further the next time, though not because anyone materially improved. Mr. Van Allen was nearly as bad as Mr. Holbrook. He was less wooden, but he sounded bored and languid, which was all wrong for the meddling Don Pedro. Isabella, with a sigh for her own maturity, decided to overlook their lackluster performances for the sake of getting through the thing. She was also eager to read for Beatrice.

She raised her chin when her turn came. "I wonder that you will still be talking, Signior Benedick: nobody marks you."

Fitz was playing Benedick and he scoffed. "What, my dear Lady Disdain! are you yet living?"

Isabella grinned. "Is it possible disdain should die while she hath such meet food to feed it as Signior Benedick? Courtesy itself must convert to disdain, if you come in her presence."

Fitz laid a hand on his heart. "Then is courtesy a turncoat. But it is certain I am loved of all ladies, only you excepted: and I would that I had not a hard heart; for, truly, I love none."

Isabella quite loved doing the scene, and the others must have enjoyed it as well, for there was general laughter as she and her brother grew increasingly dramatic. Even Mr. Darcy laughed out loud with the children when they finished.

Then it was on to further characters and meatier scenes. Mr. Hawksley sighed dramatically over his love for Hero, and Isabella nodded in approval. Maggie and Eleanor read the parts of Hero's ladies-in-waiting very respectably, for little girls, and Eleanor with rather more zest than the part called for.

"Oh," Isabella broke off somewhere in the middle of Act II. "We do not have an Antonio. I suppose it will have to be Mr. Holbrook."

He looked faintly appalled. "Wait, Miss Fitzwilliam, you've already given me three other 'small' parts since we began! If you continue at this rate I shall be in every scene of the play."

"Don't be poor-spirited, sir."

"You've already said that I lack spirit. Repeatedly, in fact, and I agree with you. It's a very just observation! I don't think you ought to give me any more roles that will displease you."

She looked at him severely. "You are not precisely good at this, but you are not hopeless. You must not make excuses."

He stiffened his shoulders. "In any case, you cannot make me be Antonio for I am already—" he checked his notes, "Verges, in this scene."

"Why didn't you say so at once?"

He cast his eyes to the ceiling.

"Who will be Antonio, then?" Isabella asked. Mr. Darcy disappeared behind a book, and Harold closed his eyes as if she could not see him if he were sleeping.

Emma spoke up. "My husband has no role."

Mr. Knightley's aristocratic brows rose. "I didn't particularly want one, my dear."

"No, this is perfect. You can be Antonio—he is my brother, you see—and you will have every scene with me. Do indulge me."

He softened as he looked at Emma and even Isabella—who was addicted to the written word and not at all interested in men—had to admit that there might be something in marriage if a man looked at you like that.

"Yes, very well, I'm Antonio," he said. "I will read from Emma's script."

"Good. We have already cut most of his lines, for they are usually only agreeing with everyone or telling Hero to listen to her father. This scene is at the masked ball when Ursula flirts with Antonio."

Mr. Knightley frowned for a moment at the implication of flirting with another lady of the house party, but then Isabella pointed to the oldest Gardiner child, Maggie. "She's Ursula. Go ahead and read, Maggie."

She giggled. "I know you well enough; you are Signior Antonio.

Mr. Knightley smiled. "At a word, I am not."

"I know you by the waggling of your head."

Mr. Knightley dutifully shook his head back and forth. "To tell you true, I counterfeit him."

"You could never do him so ill-well, unless you were the very man. Here's his hand up and down: you are he, you are he!"

"At a word, I am *not.*" Mr. Knightley pitched his voice high, and Maggie burst out laughing.

Emma bumped him with her shoulder. "I had no idea you were a dramatist! You have been holding out on me."

"I merely understood the assignment, and I have an excellent scene partner."

This made Maggie glow, but Isabella clapped her hands. "Keep going."

With one thing and another, they made it through the whole play. Isabella laid down her script happily. Somewhere around Act IV, Scene 2, Lizzy had ordered the tea to be brought. Now, by common accord, it seemed most were headed to their bedchambers.

The fresh logs placed after dinner had shrunk down to a pile of ash and a few charred bits thoroughly chewed by the fire. Mr. Holbrook lingered next to a side table with two volumes open in front of him. He seemed to be dithering over which to take up to his room.

"Do you often read before sleeping, Mr. Holbrook?" Isabella asked. "My mother says it is only a matter of time before I burn Matlock Park down with that habit."

"Yes, I do." He tapped the books. "You're not going to criticize my reading material? You seem to have strong opinions."

"I do, but frankly there are too many gentlemen who do not read at *all* for me to criticize you for reading anything."

He muttered something like, "First time today."

Isabella's mother looked over her shoulder at the books under discussion. "That can't be true, Isabella. You excoriated poor Fitz for reading *Prisoner of Chillon*."

"Fitz is my brother, I have higher standards for him than Mr. Holbrook." Her tone of voice might have gone a touch too far into condescension. A man who could not read a simple Shakespearean character was not to be trusted.

"There it is." Mr. Holbrook took up the book. "Goodnight all."

Lady Matlock paused Isabella with a hand to her elbow. "You needn't be rude to *every* young man you meet. Based on your behavior, I feel I must have been unclear on that at some point."

"I'm not! I told Mr. Holbrook I wouldn't criticize his reading, and I did not."

Lady Matlock sighed. "You are very like your father, you know. He also had strong opinions."

Fitz joined them, putting one arm around his mother and the other around his sister. "Believe it or not, Mother, you have a few strong opinions as well. I think she comes by it on both sides."

"Then how did I end up with a son as sociable as you?"

"Good question, I deserve all the credit for that."

Isabella smacked his arm. "I am going to bed. Marshalling you all into a semblance of order is exhausting."

"But you did it very well; if you were a man, you would've made a fine general."

She sighed. "I know. Greatness is a punishment when it is stifled."

{ 13 }

ALTHOUGH ELEANOR WAS PLEASED with the previous day's success, she was a little worried that Miss Crawford had not come down to dinner or to the drawing room for the first reading of the play.

She knew it was probably from the tumble Miss Crawford had had in the snow, but perhaps being stuck in the ballroom had not helped. Eleanor did not plan to repeat her trick today, but that did not mean she had to do *nothing*. There were other ways of ensuring that Uncle Fitz and Miss Crawford had time with one another.

In fact, when she realized that Miss Crawford and Uncle Fitz had voluntarily gone to the library to practice their scenes for the play just after breakfast, she realized it was not so much a matter of keeping them in, as keeping others *out*.

They had left the door open, as was proper with a lady and gentleman alone in a room, so Eleanor was able to spy out the situation with a slow walk and a quick peek.

She fetched her current book from the schoolroom and settled down on a wooden bench in an alcove just beyond the library but before the study. The book was quite good. It was titled *Travels in Hungary*, with illustrations and sixteen copperplate pictures inserted separately. She unfolded one of these pictures to examine the ancient castle of Visegrád.

Miss Darcy had a wonderful collection of books from her childhood, and she had been quite insistent that Eleanor and the other children were allowed to read them while they were here. In fact, Eleanor was so engrossed in her book, she almost forgot about her role as protector. She safely ignored four of the gentlemen, including her father, when they entered the billiard room. She didn't even register when Miss Isabella and Mrs. Van Allen went to one of the galleries, whispering and exclaiming together.

And she *almost* ignored it when Mr. Van Allen left the drawing room and approached her position. She was alerted however, by the smell of alcohol and the strong scent that he wore. Even Eleanor, at nine years old, knew it was too early in the morning to smell of alcohol.

She popped off her bench and stepped in front of him. "Good morning, Mr. Van Allen."

"Yes. Good morning." She was conscious that although she did not like Mr. Van Allen, he was more uncomfortable with her.

"Did you know that there is an ancient castle called Visegrád in Hungary? Have you been to Hungary?"

He looked reluctantly at the picture. "No. I haven't."

"Then—"

"Don't bother me just now, child."

"Of course. I am sorry. Are you looking for someone? Perhaps I can help you."

"Yes—"

"Mr. Darcy and my father and two other gentlemen went into the billiard room just there. I'm sure you could join them."

"No, I was looking for Colonel Fitzwilliam and Miss Crawford."

"Oh, yes, they were practicing in the ballroom. It is back that way, in the other wing of the house. If you cut through this gallery and take a left through the adjoining rooms you will be there." This was true, though she knew, of course, that he would not find them in the ballroom. Uncle Fitz and Miss Crawford *were* practicing in the ballroom the previous day.

"Ah. Well. Thank you." He took the cut-through of the galleries, which Eleanor and Bertie had examined earlier, finding a frightful lot of past Darcy ancestors in paintings and sculptures.

Eleanor returned to her bench, but not to read. She waited a few minutes, and then followed along after Mr. Van Allen.

She heard him enter the ballroom and speak to Miss Darcy.

"I have not seen them this morning," Miss Darcy answered. "I've been working on painting these flowers, as you see, sir."

Eleanor heard her sister Maggie's voice also. "Yes, Miss Darcy is teaching me to paint an arbor!"

"Never mind," Mr. Van Allen snapped.

Eleanor dashed back the way she'd come, listening for Mr. Van Allen's steps behind her. This was better than being a highwayman or a brigand!

The gallery route was a series of small- to medium-sized rooms that opened one into another and had been filled over many decades or perhaps centuries. They ran parallel to the length of the house.

When she got back to the other end of the galleries, she slipped out, turned, and locked the final door. Pemberley was excellent for the number of doors one could lock! A casual question had elicited the fact that the house was frequently open to tours when the family was not at home. Mrs. Reynolds explained that most portions of the house could be locked to prevent inquisitive eyes or hands.

Eleanor was not even locking Mr. Van Allen *into* a room, for he could still exit on the far side of this chain of rooms.

He tried the door, kicked it, and even said several words that Eleanor had only heard harsh, angry jarveys use in London. They were not at all *polite* words.

Eventually he gave up and stomped away.

Eleanor unlocked the door, as it would not do to leave evidence against herself. She scooped up her book to return it to the schoolroom. On the way, she heard Mr. Van Allen get waylaid by his wife and Miss Isabella, and if that wasn't perfect she didn't know what was. She had planned to have Bertie take over the next portion of misdirection, but it was not even needed. She would save it for later.

Mr. Knightley woke Emma earlier than the previous day, but still later than usual. He pulled back the drapes and allowed the winter sunshine to pierce the fine room. There was more than a foot of snow on the ground today, and much deeper in some places, but the sun had come out. It lit up the blue and cream bed hangings and reflected on the looking glass in the corner.

He sat on the side of the bed and stroked Emma's shoulder. "Emma? Did you want to get up for a luncheon?"

It had occurred to him that there could be a very simple reason for Emma's tiredness. He wondered if she had thought of it.

She blinked and covered her eyes. "It is too bright, and you are a harsh and exacting taskmaster." She paused. "Please tell me it is still morning."

"It is still morning, but it is nearing noon."

"That is not as bad as I feared." She stretched. "Ugh, I do not know why I am so tired! Lizzy will think me the laziest guest in the world."

He moved over so that she could throw back the bedclothes and put her feet on the ground, into her fur slippers.

"Have you thought there might be a reason you're so tired?"

"If this is leading up to you chastising me for staying up too late, I'll remind you that you were up just as late."

"I didn't mean that."

"I did indulge in a floating island last night, but I am not a child to be overcome by an extra dessert." She rubbed her eyes and swallowed.

"Emma!" There was a laugh in his voice. "I'm not trying to criticize you. I was suggesting that it is possible—" He felt himself blush. He was not a shy person, and he and Emma had been married over eight months, but he still felt odd suggesting that she could be with child. Not that long ago, *she* was a child. He was daily amazed that Providence had granted him the gift of Emma's love and companionship, but he was so much older and more experienced than her.

"Oh, no," she said. "You are putting on the face you wear when you say silly things about how old you are. Please do not, I am too drowsy to counter you."

"Emma, can you think of no reason you might be oddly tired and needing more rest?"

"The travel was a little fatiguing, but I did not think it would wear on me so. We are farther north, and the temperature has been very cold—now, why are you laughing?"

"Partially because you sound like your father, and partially because I don't think it is a matter of geography or atmosphere."

Emma furrowed her brow.

"Never mind. I'll leave you to get ready, and I'll send your maid up." There was still every possibility he was wrong, and he did not want to increase her hopes, or fears, without reason. He would let her come to the thought on her own.

After she had practiced with Colonel Fitzwilliam—who was unfortunately an emotive reader with a flair for acting—Mary made her way back to the drawing room to see what everyone else was busy with. She had not made very much progress in ingratiating herself with Harold and was starting to doubt the efficacy of that plan. He was so often asleep or wrapped in his own concerns; he would not be easily moved to propose.

The drawing room was indeed rather somnolent this morning. The children were elsewhere, most of the gentlemen were gone playing billiards or some such thing, and the young ladies were off working on the theatrical. Indeed, the only ladies present were Mrs. Gardiner and Lady Matlock—both of the older generation. They were ostensibly doing needlework but looked closer to a joint doze. The only gentleman was Harold Fitzwilliam, who was perusing a newspaper. There were several others folded on the small table next to him.

The light from outdoors was far brighter and more cheerful today, giving the room a lighter aspect. Or perhaps it was just that Mr. Van Allen was not present and that made Mary more sanguine for the day.

Harold tapped the pile as she seated herself nearby. "Darcy's steward brought the last three London papers this morning. Help yourself."

"Thank you, I will."

Mary did not pretend to stay up on every current issue—the Corn Laws were tiring, the news from the Continent depressing, and the latest parliamentary doings unamusing. It was generally a diatribe against either the Whigs or Tories depending on which paper one read. However, the Royal news was always worth keeping up with, not to mention the society notes and marriage announcements. She was reading these when Harold suddenly sniffed rather deeply—a suppressed sound of shock—which set him to coughing. He stopped himself with an emphatic throat clearing and wiped his watering eyes.

"Something amiss?" Mary asked.

He looked at her over the top of the paper. He was curling one edge inward as if to hide it from her view. "Er—don't know as I should be the one to tell you. None of my business."

"It pertains to me?" Then she shook her head. "Oh, of course it does. Is it more speculation about my brother Henry? You need not fear to wound me, though I did think that scandal was dying down."

"Yes, it's mostly past. Haven't heard a word at Boodle's in over a month.

"Then what has surprised you?" Harold was known to be an older and respected member of Boodle's Club in London and could reliably be depended on to know the *on-dits* of society.

"It's just a note about the Bertrams, mentions you." He winced and passed the offending sheet to her. "Probably better you see it now than hear it in a larger company."

It is to be hoped the Bertram family of Mansfield Park have arrived at calmer shores after a tumultuous year. Mariah Rushworth, nee Bertram, has disappeared from society, and now the Younger Son of Sir Thomas and Lady Bertram has wed. He was joined this Thursday last to Miss Frances Price of Portsmouth. The Price family is connected to Lady Bertram, and it is hoped to be an unexceptional, if unexciting match. The younger Mr. Bertram was rumored to make a match with London's own Mary Crawford, niece to Admiral James Crawford. Strangely, Miss Price was temporarily rumored to be engaged to Mr. Henry Crawford. It is to be hoped that Mr. Bertram and Miss Price have found consolation for their disappointments.

Mary felt a swooping sensation, an unpleasant mix of shock, nausea, and anger. She never swooned, but if she was prone to it, she would have done so. Her heart and lungs felt empty, her hands shaky, and her throat clogged. She was aware of Harold's eyes on her.

"This is... unexpected," she managed, "but I have no quarrel with the notice except for its—its rather dismissive tone towards myself and my brother. Certainly Mr. Bertram has every right to settle as he chooses; there was no understanding between us."

But there *should* have been; there *almost* was. And now he had married *Fanny*? Mary had had no idea of this. Should she have? Had she been blind? Immediately she realized that there had been indications of this on Fanny's side. Fanny was kind, good, and sweet—she would never have done anything—but she idolized her cousin.

But *he*—he had meant to propose to Mary when he came to London this summer. Hadn't he? She pressed one hand against her hot cheek.

Harold Fitzwilliam was not a sympathetic man, but he was not a monster either. He had known Miss Crawford since she was presented at seventeen, and he respected her. Intelligent, gave as good as she got, and knew how to play the game. Always dressed well, didn't giggle incessantly or make stupid demands... she was a 'right one,' as his brother would say.

He didn't want to increase her awkwardness. He took up his paper and looked at it studiously; the only sympathetic action he was capable of.

Mary understood.

"Thank you. Please excuse me." She rose as gracefully as ever and quietly let herself out of the room, only making a brief excuse to a half-awake Lady Matlock.

Mary needed solitude, a moment for reflection.

Unfortunately, she got Mr. Van Allen. He was in the hallway, opening and shutting one of the gallery doors with a forbidding scowl on his face.

"Mary, there you are." He slammed the door one final time. "I was looking for you."

"I have been in the library, but I don't feel well. I'm going to lie down."

"No, hang it all, I've been looking for nearly an hour—"

Mary was fixated on her news, but this made her lip curl. "In this house? I was not hidden, sir."

"Blast it, I know, but first it was a castle, then it was the blasted gallery and what's her name painting—then that little boy with the bulging eyes must needs follow me with eighty questions. And I swear this door was locked." He finished this recital of his wrongs by opening and slamming it again.

Mary stared at him. "Perhaps *you* ought to lie down. You are making less sense than usual. How much have you had to drink this morning?"

His face was already flushed unbecomingly. He wrapped a hand around her wrist. "Not that much. Now, step into the study—"

"Nonsense. I am going upstairs to my room. If you have anything to say to me, you can do it later. In company."

"What are you going to do, make a little fuss? Claim I am bothering you? I will remind you, Miss Crawford, that you have a reputation. Do you think they'll believe you're innocent? It is only your encouragement that has brought me here."

"I did not encourage you; not—" Mary faltered. She *had* flirted with him, she had allowed a stolen kiss or two. "But *not* since you were married."

"A virtuous woman wouldn't have to make that distinction. You can pretend to be indifferent, but I know what you are. And so do these people. Now, Mary, damned if I don't *deserve*—"

What he thought he deserved he did not say, though she could guess, because little Eleanor came around the corner with her book.

She was surely too young to extrapolate much from their positions, and she artlessly approached them with her book. "Hello, Miss Crawford. I have been reading this delightful book about Hungary. Have you ever been there?"

"None of us *care* about Hungary or castles," Mr. Van Allen snapped.

Mary jerked her wrist away from him, sliding away from the wall he had pressed her up against. "That is no way to speak to a child. And no, Eleanor, I have not been to Hungary. I am not feeling well right now, but perhaps you could tell me all about it later today."

"Oh, yes, thank you!"

Eleanor stood by while Mary went to the central stairs. She stared without blinking at Mr. Van Allen who made a disgusted noise and turned away.

Mary was preoccupied in thinking that Van was right. Based on her limited experience, no one would believe her if she claimed Van Allen was pestering or harassing her. Her reputation of being a little *fast* was too well-known. No one would believe that Mr. Van Allen was doing all this under his own volition despite decided *discouragement* from her.

Even at Mansfield Park, where she had been much attached to Fanny and Edmund, the parents, the sisters... there had been no background of kind, sincere people for her to gain experience of. Although Mary might be maligning the character of the others in this house party, her ignorance of the behavior of good people in large groups was complete. She could only act on what she knew.

{ 14 }

SOME HOURS LATER, MARY ROSE from her chair by the fire. She could not stay in her room *all day*, nor would it be good or healthy for her to do so.

The fire in her room had served as a backdrop for many tangled thoughts and images for a troubled afternoon. The fire had held a might-have-been ceremony between herself and Edmund and a could-have-been image of his house at Thornton Lacy becoming her home and kingdom.

The embers had sparked at memories of the brief kisses she had shared with him. The leaping yellow and orange flames had been a counterpoint to her memories of rides with him, dances with him, jokes and debates with him.

As it lessened, she slipped out of the past and into the future, imagining him living out his life with Fanny. Fanny! Mary had thought she knew them both so well. She had loved Edmund, but she had also loved Fanny in her way. She had been the chiefest supporter of her brother's proposals to Fanny. She had hoped he would secure her a sister she genuinely valued and enjoyed.

Instead, Edmund and Fanny.

Mary could see how it happened. Fanny must have been in love with him for years. Fanny's own standoffishness with herself was now explained. Mary had always chalked it up to her shyness and reserve, the difference in their upbringing, or Mary's free manners... but it had also been this.

Mary had tried to befriend Fanny while also pursuing the man Fanny loved. Of course Fanny had never truly warmed up to her. Their friendship had been even more one-sided than Mary could have guessed.

Mary shook her head. She had known Edmund was lost to her after their last, explosive conversation. It surprised her that this should have cut her on the raw. She should be happy for them, perhaps, but she could not have such perfect resignation yet.

Still, after two hours of contemplation, a few tears, and—if anyone had been there to hear it—some grinding of teeth, she was ready to rejoin the guests of the house.

She poured water from her pitcher into the wash basin. It was cold—very cold—but she pressed it to her face repeatedly. Tears, redness, oil—all would be washed away.

She pressed the linen hand-towel to her face and avoided harsh rubbing. Even in grief a responsible woman remembered her complexion.

It was mid-afternoon now, and from her window she saw the children and several adults heading across the snowy expanse to the sledding hill. At this distance she could not identify each person in the expedition, but there was Mr. Hawksley's somewhat round figure, the four children strung out like beads in descending size, and Colonel Fitzwilliam's straight figure bringing up the rear with a sled.

When she descended, her luck was in. Only Mr. and Mrs. Knightley, and Lizzy and Mr. Darcy were in the drawing room. She did not have to bear Alicia's glares, Isabella's insatiability, or any of the gentlemen's gallantries.

The two couples were laughing. Even Mr. Darcy and Mr. Knightley looked positively relaxed in enjoyment with their good friends.

They welcomed Mary, though Lizzy was in the middle of a story. "No sooner had we seen the gypsies and barely interacted with the poor folk, than the silly Miss Bickerton screams and runs directly up hill. She went off the path, through brambles and bracken, as if a swarm of bees were behind her. Then poor Harriet—who at least had the good sense not to run—was nearly overcome with mortification when the gypsies surrounded us. As well they might, we were offering more of a show than they ever did."

Emma laughed. "Poor Harriet! She is much more confident than she used to be. You should see her coming into town with her husband and her baby, she is so proud and happy."

Mr. Knightley smiled. "That day with the gypsies must be when Darcy came across you. He came to tell me of the event just afterward, and looking back, I do not think I have ever seen him so discontent."

"I was bitterly jealous," Darcy admitted. "I was leaving town, you were engaged; I had nothing to do with the entire matter, no reason to stay, and I resented it."

Lizzy raised his hand to her lips for a quick kiss. "My poor Mr. Darcy suffered dreadfully, but at least I did not make him wait long. After I returned to London I all but proposed the first time he came to call."

He furrowed his brow. "That is not how I recall it. You were never pushing, never forward."

She patted his hand. "I am glad that is how *you* recall it."

The others laughed at her arch tone, and Mary could not help but marvel at them. She had known Mr. Knightley and Mrs. Darcy had been briefly engaged—that had been its own brief scandal—but she had supposed it would be tacitly left in the past, not mentioned at all. There was such trust and good humor on display here, it was quite breathtaking.

Mr. Darcy smiled. "I suppose most hints are lost on me, so I appreciated your clarity."

"Clarity—what an excellent word!" Lizzy said. "The ill-disposed would call it 'wretched impertinence' or a 'dreadful lack of tact.' But we must not be too ridiculous, or Miss Crawford will think we are quite mad."

She disclaimed any such thought.

Emma leaned against her husband's shoulder, making herself comfortable. "It was a whirlwind winter, and no mistake. However, it ended happily, and I have the relief of knowing that Harriet is well despite my mistakes, so I am at peace with it."

"How is Harriet?" Lizzy asked.

"Oh, excellent! She has the sweetest little baby boy. His face is as round as a saucer. The Martins are ever so pleased, and she was beaming when I last saw her. Her early days were a bit trying—" Emma broke off and changed color. "Oh my."

Mary's sharp eyes saw Emma's hand clutch her husband's knee.

Emma tried to continue. "But—but she is well. Have you heard from your sisters lately?"

The conversation moved on, but Mary observed Emma look up at her husband in question. He smiled tenderly. Emma's face was a picture of surprise, consternation, and pleasure. Mr. Knightley subtly shifted her, tucking his arm around her shoulders and cuddling her closer to him.

Lizzy was giving an update on her sister Jane and Mr. Bingley, and Mary forced her focus that direction. The moment of realization between Mr. Knightley and Emma was too personal to intrude.

Mary felt the sting of tears, and she had to widen her eyes and press on the corner once or twice to force them back. Perhaps she was vulnerable because of her recent news. The sight of such a harmonious marriage, full of love, trust, and adoration was quite painful.

Watching Darcy and Lizzy was almost as bad. Their dynamic was different than Knightley and Emma—a little more teasing on her side, a little more reserve on his—but it was no less happy. The fact that Mr. Darcy felt no fear of Lizzy's attachment to Mr. Knightley was a firm statement of trust.

It was almost shockingly painful to sit with two such blissfully happy couples.

Mary smiled, and replied, and asked questions, but she had to remove herself before too long. She went into the music room where her harp had been removed, at her request. If she wished to play it during the day, she didn't want to silence everyone in the drawing room. She removed the cover and sat with a relieved breath. Music was a medium in which she could lose herself and forget her fears of an unhappy future.

She plucked the first few strings tentatively, checking the tuning, and then began to play in earnest. She played a piece she had memorized years ago. The distance of time made it difficult. Several times she had to pause and begin a run again more slowly. Such practice did her good; it fixed her mind on notes, chords, and patterns, not marital felicity or the lack thereof.

Eleanor returned from the snowy outing in great spirits. Her mother came to the room she and Maggie shared and helped them change out of their wet things.

"How you got snow *inside* your drawers, I do not know," her mother said. "Did you use a sled or not?"

"We did," Eleanor explained, "but sometimes we rolled off of it."

She shivered and moved closer to the grate of the fireplace in their room. It had been freshly stoked in each room for those who had just come in, and Eleanor was very thankful.

She and Maggie stripped off their wet things, and their mother hung them on the back of a chair that she'd moved close to the fire. Fresh, dry drawers, stockings, petticoats, and short dresses were soon donned. They each had a shawl, given by their cousin Jane, and their mother wrapped them up well. "You can take them off when your lips are no longer blue."

After Maggie told their mother how Miss Isabella had nearly tumbled into the lake with one lucky—or unlucky—slide, Eleanor's mind returned to what she'd seen earlier.

"Mother, what does it mean if a man grabs a woman?"

"Excuse me?"

"If he grabs her arm." Eleanor latched onto Maggie's wrist to demonstrate. "I might give Bertie or Pip a sharp kick in the shin if they did that to me. But I have never seen Father do that to you."

"Am I correct in assuming you saw this happen here at Pemberley?"

"Yes."

"Most likely it was in jest. Men and women, particularly husbands and wives, sometimes tease one another—"

"But they both looked angry."

"Hm. Maggie, dear, would you go to Bertie and Pip and tell them to meet us in the school room?"

"Yes, Mother."

When Maggie was gone, Mrs. Gardiner sat down with her younger daughter. "Now, what did you see? Perhaps you misunderstood what happened. You are quick and observant for a nine-year-old, but there is much about adult relationships you don't know."

"It was Mr. Van Allen and Miss Crawford."

"Oh?"

"Yes. I like her pro*dig*iously."

"I'm glad, my sweet, she seems a pleasant, intelligent young woman."

"But she was in the hall with Mr. Van Allen and he was holding on tight to her wrist. I distracted them with my book, and she jerked her hand away like this." Eleanor held onto her own wrist and jerked her hand downward toward her thumb. "She went right up to her room, and she did not look as if she was teasing."

"Ah, I see." Her mother looked thoughtful for a moment, then smoothed Eleanor's hair gently. "Thank you for telling me. I will keep an eye on them, but you should not worry yourself. You have done your duty and now you can be easy."

"Yes, Mother. Will we be allowed to come down after supper, like yesterday evening?"

"I believe so, yes. Please be on your best behavior. Even if you do not like Mr. Van Allen—or any of the guests!—I hope I have taught you to act respectfully."

"Of course," Eleanor agreed. If she had to lock, block, or misdirect Mr. Van Allen again, she would do so respectfully.

"Thank you, my dear." Mrs. Gardiner went downstairs again, concerned but blissfully ignorant of her daughter's plans.

Mr. Knightley followed Emma into her room and closed the door. She spun around and her hands were pressed to her cheeks. "Do you think it could be? A—a baby?"

He put one hand over hers, his thumb stroking her cheek. "It is certainly possible. I was biting my tongue and all you could talk about was weather and geography."

Emma's laugh bubbled out of her. "That is very unfair. I am not accustomed to ascribing every indisposition to such a cause."

"I should think not." He wrapped his arm around her waist and pulled her close, cradling her against his chest. "I know Mrs. Weston was everything to you, but perhaps she didn't explain—"

"No, she did! You need not explain it all. I am merely lost in wonder." She suddenly gasped and cringed closer to him. "My *father*."

Mr. Knightley stroked her back. "He'll be worried, but your sister has given him five grandchildren. He is at least somewhat used to the danger."

"No, you cannot have thought! With my sister in London, all he could do was worry from afar. He never saw her increase, never saw her unwell, or—or in pain. With me always before him—oh, I cannot imagine."

Mr. Knightley stilled. "Perhaps we could hide for nine months."

"Far away."

"Very far."

Emma sighed. "We shall have to face up to it. In fact, if my sums are correct, maybe it will only be six or seven months."

"Truly?"

"You criticize my mathematics? Now?"

He laughed, holding her tighter. "Emma, my dear pest, that was not a criticism, and you know it. I am surprised."

"I have never been perfectly regular, so I am not certain... but Mrs. Weston did teach me to count."

"Your father will have his doctor to visit you every day."

"We should move poor Perry into the house. Pay him a stipend."

"I am not made of money, my dear."

Emma laughed and then sighed. "I love you, Mr. Knightley."

"I love you, Emma. A thousand times more than I can express."

{ 15 }

LORD MATLOCK WAS A LAZY MAN, he did not deny or excuse or glory in it, it was simply who he was. On the other hand, he would do a fair bit for his friends.

Witness his efforts in that stupid duel last summer! He bestirred himself when needed, and it was his doing that a good surgeon had been on sight to help when Mr. Darcy took that ricocheted bullet.

This instance required even less of him, except a little presence of mind. After Miss Crawford left the drawing room, he'd extracted the offending page of the newspaper, folded it, and tucked it in his inner jacket pocket. There was no need for the whole blasted house party to read about Miss Crawford's disappointment. An impudent and insulting article, but that was to be expected. The *haute ton* loved scurrilous gossip, and the Mansfield Park affair—as some were calling it—was ripe with it. Encompassing as it did the fall of Maria Rushworth, the elopement of Julia Bertram, the duel involving Tom Bertram, and the destruction of both the Crawfords' expectations... well, it was a miracle the article was as restrained as it was.

He didn't think of it again until he was changing his clothes for supper. His valet helped him out of the jacket, then frowning, withdrew the newsprint from his pocket.

"You need this, sir?"

"Eh, what's that? Oh, no, it's trash."

The valet laid it next to his shaving kit. "I will dispose of it later then, sir. Your waistcoat?"

"Let's go with the turquoise stripe."

Darcy was less of a high stickler than he had been—probably his wife's influence—but at least they still dressed for dinner. Harold shuddered to think how casual Darcy would be in twenty years.

Harold was lazy, but he was not savage. The doings of the upper class in London were what he was born and bred to, and he was fastidious in matters of dress and table.

At his country seat, Matlock Park, everything was done just as he liked. Harold had no great desire to marry and add a Lady Matlock to the estate. His mother would gladly relinquish the title and become the *Dowager* Lady Matlock in a trice if he would only wed and provide England with a new countess, but he was not motivated.

No woman had ever tempted him. Harold was quite content that Fitz should inherit the estate after him, or failing him, Isabella. She'd probably create some sort of blue-stocking retreat and fill it with women of letters and no fortune, but she wasn't a bad sort. Many of his friends had young sisters with far less in their heads.

Of course, Harold wasn't *devoted* to the idea of passing it to Fitz; if any woman ever took his fancy enough to go to the trouble of marriage, Harold would happily cut him out. None had. Nor was Harold tempted by Miss Crawford. He liked and respected her, but marriage held no great appeal. She would not contribute much to his comfort, and he felt no desire to have her at hand for the next fifty-odd years.

He rather suspected that she'd set her thoughts on him. The fact that she'd spent more than a spare hour or two sitting quietly in that alcove with him while he read—or dozed more likely—was a clear indicative. He was indolent, while she had always been described as lively to a fault.

He didn't resent her for her efforts. It made sense for her to snag an earl if she could, but he wouldn't be the one. He wished her well, but not that well. She'd do better with Fitz, as a matter of fact. He was a good chap, and he needed a fortune. Even if he did inherit Matlock Park, Harold had no intention of dying for some time, so that was no immediate prospect.

His valet paused by the door. "That's all, sir, unless you wish for help with your cravat."

Harold realized that with his rather unusual cogitations, he had prepared for dinner faster than normal. Rush of any sort was anathema to him. He tied his cravat with care and was satisfied with the production. "That'll be all."

When his valet departed, Harold sat down before his fire and put his hands on his belly. A good moment for a brief snooze before supper.

He had only just entered into this when a sharp knock on the door roused him. "Eh, what?"

Fitz pushed the door opened and entered.

"You know, the army gave you a sad disregard for privacy," Harold said.

Fitz waved that aside. "Don't be finicky."

"Well, what is it? Why am I thus imposed upon?"

Fitz seemed to lose a little steam now that he was in Harold's room. "I, er, I spent the morning practicing the play with Miss Crawford."

"Silly thing, theatricals. A great lot of work for something one can see done better on any stage in London."

"Yes, but we aren't in London. It's... diverting. An activity for those who don't like to be idle."

"If that was a hint, I scoff at it. I enjoy being idle, and I don't like plays."

"I don't care about your opinion of the play. It is about Miss Crawford."

"She is the sort who enjoys theatricals. Perhaps that's part of the reason I don't want her."

Fitz looked a little taken aback.

This time it was Harold who waved his hand. He'd forgotten Fitz wasn't privy to his musings while he dressed. "Never mind. What is it? Do cut line."

"That is... part of it, as a matter of fact. I was wondering if you'd any intentions there. She said something to that effect."

"Did she? Don't seem like her to make up stories."

"No, no." Fitz fiddled with Harold's strait razor. "It was merely that young Maggie came around and said something embarrassing. She accidentally called Miss Crawford by the wrong name, as Miss Fitzwilliam. The little girl stuttered about for a moment, before blurting out that Mary Fitzwilliam would be a very nice name; wouldn't she and Uncle Fitz be so handsome together, etc. It was harmless, childish teasing—and Miss Crawford laughed and said, 'Not with *this* Fitzwilliam.' It was just repartee, a slight set down to Maggie for her forwardness, but it did get me to wondering."

"Sounds like a set-down to me. No need to lock up your limited brains in an imaginary puzzle."

Fitz rolled his eyes and tossed the razor down next to the brush. "Fine, fine."

He leaned over and looked at the newsprint. "I say, what's this?" He picked it up, crackling the paper open. "It mentions Miss Crawford."

"My valet must've forgotten to take it away with him. It was supposed to go in the rubbish. Oh well, yours are not the eyes I was keeping it from."

Fitz made short work of reading the article. "Was she really going to marry this undistinguished country parson and retire from London? I don't believe it."

"I do not know how you have been home nearly a year and still so ignorant of current events."

"I read other parts of the newspaper."

"Again, if that is a hint, I scoff at it. You may think me a sad gossip, but I know what needs to be known. If it weren't for my gossiping ways, there might've been a less capable second at that duel with Darcy."

Fitz refolded the paper, reading the article again. "Yes, I admit it. But this is surprising. I suppose this man, Edmund Bertram, had a near escape if she was serious about him."

"A near escape? That is the least chivalrous thing I've heard you say."

"Maybe I was overly harsh. She is an unconscionable flirt, but perhaps he was willing to put up with that."

"Unconscionable?" Harold considered. She had apparently "set her cap" at him, but that had mainly involved spending quiet moments with him and exchanging quips at dinner. "She adapts herself to her company, better than most."

"She's made poor Mrs. Van Allen's visit rather trying, and I observed that dynamic before ever we left London. Miss Crawford has the ability to send every gentleman she meets into knots, and the Van Allen situation is even worse. I told Darcy he was an idiot for inviting them."

"He was; that's true. Van Allen is..." Harold made a gross noise in his throat. "I don't say I blame Van for tiring of his new wife, but instead of striking up a flirtation with a well-placed widow or unhappy peeress, or even a saucy opera dancer, he must needs persecute Miss Crawford. And while she was on a visit to them. Very bad ton."

Fitz was rather disgusted by most of the options his brother put forth, but he ignored that for now. "Persecute Miss Crawford? How can you say so? She seems to welcome his presence, never gives the slightest hint of discomfort. She laughs, she deflects, she teases... in short, she flirts with him."

Harold squeezed the bridge of his nose. "Did you interrupt my doze to persecute me with your stupidity? Do they not teach observation in the army? She is a proud woman. She does not want pity. She tells him *no* in every way a polite woman can, and I suspect speaks the word quite plainly in private. I do wonder how you became a colonel, sometimes."

"But if that's true... it's dreadful."

"Welcome to society."

"And is she being annoyed under Darcy's roof? We ought to send Van Allen packing if so."

"She's well able to care for herself. A proud duo, she and her brother. I suspect they'll always land on their feet."

Fitz ran the shaving brush back and forth over the back of his hand. "I will see what I can observe with this new perspective. I'm not yet convinced."

"Do as you will, only leave me alone to—oh, blast. There is the chime striking seven."

Fitz patted his brother's shoulder. "You can doze just as well after the meal."

It was after supper that Mary sought some further time alone. She had put on a good face after hearing the news, spent a trying hour with what might be the two happiest couples in Britain, and then been most pleasant and lively at supper.

She really could not ask more of herself at present. Later she would be required to read for the play again, but until the gentlemen joined them, she had a respite. The ladies had gone to the larger of the drawing rooms, and she excused herself again to the music room, where she might play the harp.

Mary calculated that she was safe from masculine interruption while the gentlemen remained at the table, drinking their port or Scotch. Still, she protected herself by inviting Eleanor to join her.

Eleanor monologued happily about Hungary, detailing the history, culture, and—slightly misunderstood—geography she had gleaned from her book.

Mary listened with half an ear, while also playing scales and arpeggios she had not practiced in far too long.

She had gone halfway into a piece, played *largo* and *pianissimo* out of respect for Eleanor's impromptu lecture, when she realized Eleanor had fallen silent.

Mary's fingers stilled. "I'm sorry, did I stop attending? What was that last part?"

"It's fine, Miss Crawford, you already listened more even than my mother." She chewed her lip. "Are you... unhappy?"

"No, not at all. I love playing the harp, and I am happy to have your company."

"Ye-es. I hope so. Only sometimes when Father is traveling, Mother will tuck us into bed or walk with us to Regent's Park and she is *happy,* but also *not* happy."

Mary resumed playing. "You're a clever little girl, but you do not need to worry about me. My life has been easy since I was a child. I have nothing to complain about."

"What about Mr. Van Allen?"

Mary's hands struck a discordant noise, and she flattened her fingers against the strings to silence the ugliness. "What about him?"

"I don't know; only you said you had nothing to complain of, but I think you do. I don't mind. Usually the boys complain to Maggie because she is very good at listening to them—better than me—but I do not mind listening."

"That is very kind of you, but one adult should not complain about another to a child." She saw more questions rising in Eleanor's face and she hurried on. "Nor do I have anything to complain about. Please do not think so." *Please do not tell your parents or relatives anything either,* Mary thought, but she was not so far gone as to ask Eleanor to keep a secret. Mary had realized at some point that every adult who asked her to keep a secret as a child had been using her. There was the tutor who'd kissed her—"Don't tell, Mary, no one would understand what we have; they would blame me."

There was her uncle, when she'd unintentionally caught him with his mistress, "Don't tell you aunt, my dear, it would only hurt her. It's our secret."

And Van Allen, of course, "We don't have to tell Alicia; it can be a secret."

At least her brother Henry—though he had arguably destroyed both their lives with his carelessness—had never asked her to keep it a secret. He had kept his own counsel and when he asked for her forgiveness, he had done it sincerely.

Good heavens, her brother! Did he know about Fanny and Edmund's marriage? Had he seen that vile note in the newspaper? Henry would be devastated. He knew Fanny was lost to him, just as Mary had known Edmund was lost to her, but their marriage was a final nail in the coffin. How ironic that she and her brother had fallen in love with two people who ended up with each other.

She and her brother had always been two peas in a pod. They had been a duo, defending and loving each other in the midst of their uncle's less than affectionate household. Their partnership had continued when they came of age and joined the London scene. It had even lasted when she'd left her uncle's house to avoid his new mistress. Henry had accompanied her to their half-sister near Mansfield Park.

It was the brouhaha with the Bertrams that had sundered them: namely Henry's stupid and careless affair with Maria. Perhaps their closeness was why she had not blamed him as she ought for his part in it. And perhaps her close identification with him was why she did not trust herself anymore. Whatever crimes her brother was capable of, she must also be capable of them.

She had wanted to excuse his behavior because she wanted an excuse for herself. Edmund's round condemnation of her brother had felt like a personal attack.

Mary grimaced at her old self as her fingers continued to pluck the strings. She had gone over many of these thoughts before. It was as well-worn a path as her favorite prelude, but she had never reached this end before. Her brother *had* done very wrong and broken more than one trust. She did not want to be like that; she did not have to be. She wanted to be trustworthy, good, even *pure*—the word Van Allen used to insult her.

She was not pretending. No one, not Mr. Van Allen or Edmund or even Henry, could make her follow her brother's path.

Mary brought her song to a close and smiled at Eleanor. "You have been very patient. Would you like a small lesson?"

"Yes, please, Miss Crawford."

"Come and sit here, just in front of me."

Even Mary smiled as Mr. Gardiner read Borachio's part of *Much Ado About Nothing*.

He sat with his daughter Eleanor perched on his knee. "Know that I have tonight wooed Margaret, the Lady Hero's gentlewoman, by the name of Hero."

He solemnly kissed his daughter's hand, who was playing the part of the maid. She giggled.

"She leaned me out at her mistress' chamber-window," he said, "and bid me a thousand times goodnight. I tell this tale vilely! I should first tell thee how the prince, Claudio, planted and placed and possessed by my master Don John, saw afar off in the orchard this amiable encounter."

Eleanor giggled again and waved a handkerchief and blew a kiss, pretending to be the maid "wooed" by Borachio.

Mary chuckled. Mr. Gardiner and Eleanor had certainly destroyed the salaciousness of the scene. The play she and Henry had attempted at Mansfield Park had been very different. Fanny had thought theatricals dangerous and problematic, but this one was certainly rendered innocent by the manner it was performed. What would Fanny think of it?

Mary pressed the thought away. She and Fanny were no longer on writing terms. Perhaps someday.

The party laughed at Mr. Gardiner and his daughter's theatrics, and the practice went on. The two villains were caught. Borachio and his friend Conrad, who was played by a much put-upon Mr. Holbrook, were accosted by two very small but militant watchmen in the persons of Bertie and Pip.

"We charge you, in the prince's name, stand!" cried Pip.

Bertie held out a wooden sword he had brought down from the nursery. "Call up the right master constable. We have here recovered the most dangerous piece of knavery that ever was known in the commonwealth."

Pip planted his small boots firmly. "And one Deformed is one of them: I know him; a' wears a lock."

Mr. Holbrook, the deformed one of the scene, sighed and finished it off.

"Don't *sigh,*" scolded Isabella, their director. "You sound like a bellows. Conrad is insolent and bold and mocking."

"He's not the only one," Mr. Holbrook murmured.

"I heard that," Isabella said. She must not have wanted to undo the group's progress, however, for she let it go.

Mary was soon back in, reading for Beatrice. Isabella had suggestions for her also, and all too often, Mary was reading opposite Colonel Fitzwilliam or Mr. Van Allen as Don Pedro. Even worse were all the scenes she read with Alicia, who was playing Hero. Her glare was palpable.

Isabella even noticed her antipathy and commented. "Hero is very grateful to her devoted cousin Beatrice—they do not have a contentious relationship."

Alicia lowered her eyes and nodded.

Mary took the opportunity to pass the book to Isabella. "I really think you ought to do Beatrice! Everyone says you did so well during that first read through."

Isabella blushed. "No, no, I am the director and already Don John, though he does not have as many scenes since we have cut some. But I don't have any ambition to be one of the main players—"

"Please, you would be doing me a favor. You can play opposite your brother and Mrs. Van Allen. It is perfect. I daresay we could give Don John to Mr. Holbrook."

That young man choked.

"I'm only jesting," Mary said. "I know you could not take another role. I could do it."

Alicia warmly seconded this exchange and was soon followed by several others who encouraged Isabella to take it—"if Miss Crawford was certain she preferred a smaller role."

Miss Crawford was certain.

Only the children were vocal nay-sayers. "But—but—" Eleanor cried, "it was supposed to be Uncle Fitz and Miss Crawford."

Mary gave her a stern look and shook her head. Eleanor slumped, defeated.

Eventually Isabella succumbed. "Oh, very well. I won't deny Beatrice is my favorite character by far."

Mary sat back happily. Most of her new scenes were with Mr. Gardiner or Mr. Holbrook, much more pleasant for everyone.

Mary's peace was only shaken later than night when Mrs. Gardiner pulled her aside. "I must say, Miss Crawford, you are excellent with children! You have quite convinced my children of your worth, and you silenced Eleanor's lapse of manners with only a look. I'm sure you will be a wonderful mother someday."

Mary had *never* received such a compliment before, if compliment it was.

Mrs. Gardiner winced. "Perhaps that is not for me to say—and of course, I know in much of the *beau monde* the idea of motherhood is more of a necessary evil than in my circles—"

Mary cut her off. "Thank you, Mrs. Gardiner, of course I take it as a compliment. I haven't given much thought to motherhood, but I can admit that your children have made me less afraid of the state."

{16}

THE FOLLOWING DAYS FOUND a more sedate pattern for Mary. A pattern of small chats, of excursions into a continuing snowy wonderland, of harp lessons with Eleanor, and practices for the play. Mary took care to avoid tête-à-tête situations with Mr. Van Allen. She ignored or excused the glares and snide comments from Alicia. She sat with Harold, though her hopes of him were beginning to lessen.

She wrote to her brother about the Bertrams. She wrote to Lady Stornaway about a visit.

She watched the growing flirtation between Isabella and Mr. Holbrook and wondered if they realized what was between them. She even felt old and jaded, as she watched Mr. Holbrook's banter grow more bold and his seldom-seen smile grow more common. Perhaps she was as old as Alicia had accused her of being.

Mary also, inexplicably, found certain passages of Pemberley blocked to her. There seemed to be no rhyme or reason to it, just mysteriously blocked doors from furniture that shifted on its own, rugs that turned up without explanation, and keys that disappeared from locks. She even heard Mr. Van Allen haranguing Darcy's butler about the stupid house and how it took him thirty minutes—*thirty minutes!*—to make his way to breakfast. Mary had just been glad she was finished by the time he made it down.

The Darcy's butler had been dignified and apologetic, though he explained that he had gone through the whole house and found not a stitch or a footstool out of place. "It might be the children," he'd offered.

Lizzy, who had walked in on this, had frowned. "Do we have any reason to suspect them of being naughty? I have never known them to play such tricks."

The butler had spread his hands. "Then I can only think, ma'am, with so many people in the house, that it is accidental. One person moves a footstool to their liking, another absently locks the gallery door when they leave..."

The matter had been dropped then, though Mary had also seen Lizzy take the butler aside. "No one blames *you,*" she said, "least of all me. Only please make sure the servants know not to lock *any* doors. Even ones we might normally lock in the evening—the galleries and the larder and so on—just to be on the safe side. And please have Mrs. Reynolds take up all the keys she can find, in case it *is* the children, though I do not at all think so."

The man left satisfied with his mistress's orders, and Mary could only assume the instructions were carried out. The house still seemed to have a mind of its own.

The end of their stay was coming upon them. The theatrical was planned for that very night, and the ball would be the following night. Lizzy had been busy receiving acceptance notes from the other landed families of the neighborhood, and she was quite pleased at the number that would hopefully attend.

Snow was still on the ground, and two nights ago it had snowed again, dumping fresh powder. The little Gardiners were in an ecstasy of joy over days of sledding, and even Mary had begun to accompany them again, after her muscles stopped protesting her first trip. The adults were comfortably expecting the roads to be better in time for the ball and their own trips home.

The strange proclivities of the house had not seriously impeded Mary until she was coming in from the latest snow expedition. She had planned to rest a little and then help Georgiana and Isabella with last minute preparations for the theatrical. However, she'd lagged behind the group, investigating the kitchen garden.

It was surrounded by a wall which had mostly protected it from heavy snow. The garden was divided into four quarters, with a small pool in the center, like a Persian garden. The pool was not frozen, for the walls kept the wind and some of the cold out. The stones soaked up the sun's heat and slowly dispersed it. The garden was mostly barren at this time of year, but she noticed some white flowers growing right up against the wall, delicate things that seemed too lovely to grow against the mortar and rock of the wall. Then she noticed that there were a few beds that'd been cleared of snow and held some straggled green shoots. She didn't know what they were, but any green at all was impressive.

"Miss Crawford?" It was Colonel Fitzwilliam, come to fetch her.

"You did not need to wait for me. I was admiring Pemberley's kitchen garden."

"Ah, yes. I see some hearty root vegetables are still in the ground."

"Is that what these are? I do not know much about gardening."

"Yes. These might be turnips or radishes. Those are definitely onion."

"How knowledgeable you are."

"Well, we were well fed when we were situated in a town, but it's a rare officer that hasn't enjoyed an onion or two on a long march."

"Ah."

"It is cold, Miss Crawford. We should head back inside." He ground his foot against a clump of snow perched on one of the stones of the path. It crunched dryly.

"Yes, of course. Though the walls make it a little warmer in here, don't they?"

"They do, that's true. At Croome Court, in Worcestershire, they've built a heated wall for their kitchen garden. There are five furnaces set into it."

She followed him up the path to the center pool and then toward the door. "What an enormous amount of fuel that must take."

"Indeed, but they have grapes and other fruit year around."

They both paused as they noticed the wooden door to the kitchen garden.

"That was open earlier, wasn't it?" he asked.

"Yes, I'm sure of it. I saw those white flowers as I was walking past."

"Hm." He tried the door and went still. "I daresay you will not be surprised if I say it won't open?"

Mary brought her fist up to rest against her mouth. There was a deep silence, broken only by the chirping of one brave bird. "But of *course* it won't open. I'm sure there is some gardener who locks up daily and did not see us in here."

"That strains credulity."

She gave him a withering look. "I know."

"It was windy earlier."

"I would describe it as breezy at most. Not enough to blow a door shut and *lock* it."

"It does have a little give. It feels as if it is hitting something." The door thumped repeatedly against something solid and heavy as he tried to shove it open.

"Did you tell anyone you were coming in here?" Mary asked.

"No. I noticed after the children went in that you were not behind me, as I thought. I turned back alone."

"I suppose someone will miss us soon. They will at least miss us from the theatrical."

"Or the door will inexplicably open before that. I swear I have never believed in ghosts, but I am starting to. Van Allen said something about it yesterday and I laughed at him. Maybe I ought to have listened."

"The Pemberley ghost? Is there such a thing?"

"Have you *met* my cousin Darcy? He is the least likely man in the world to encourage a haunting."

"Supposedly ghosts don't come for encouragement, but rather the reverse. Every ghost likes a good scream."

"But that is the kind of encouragement I mean. Darcy would never scream. He would analyze it, question it, and probably offend it in some fashion by comparing it negatively to other ghosts."

Mary laughed.

Colonel Fitzwilliam jiggled the door again. "There is definitely something blocking it."

"Perhaps it is our dignity. It is certainly not in here."

"I really must learn not to leave mine lying about." He *thunked* his shoulder heavily against the wooden door. Still no headway.

Mary wrapped her arms around herself. The kitchen garden was slightly warmer, but not *very* warm. The water was not frozen, but only just. There was a whisper of wind through the dry leaves, the rustle of dry stalks, and the rubbing of barren limbs against one another. The ground was mostly clear, but some clumps of snow clung to life, dotting the rectangular garden like half-melted croquet balls.

"We should probably walk about, to keep our blood warm," Fitz suggested.

Mary had no fault to find with the program, and they diligently walked up and down the paths. She sulkily stomped on any snowy clumps in their path, and by the third circuit, most of them were flattened ice-slush markers of her passage.

By the end of half an hour, or perhaps closer to an hour—she was not sure—Mary was completely disillusioned with the kitchen garden and more chilled than she'd expected.

Fitz eyed her shivering form, her arms tightly wrapped around her waist. Her cheeks had spots of color, but she looked miserably cold.

"The lack of sun doesn't help," he said. "The walls are casting too much shadow, but there's a spot of sunlight on the far side."

They stood in the bit of sun, turning themselves like roast goose and not even worrying about the turnips under their feet until the line of sunlight went up the wall and out of their reach. Mary plucked one of the white flowers with a pinch and twist. She spun it in shivering fingers. "What a grand time we are having."

Fitz looked at the flower in her hands. One of the fingers of her white glove was now green-stained with the juice of the stem. Her teeth were beginning to chatter.

Fitz went back to try the door again. "No luck, I'm afraid. At any rate, it must be after four. Someone will be along to look for us soon."

"This is s-so st-stupid. And I am n-not that cold. I do not know why I am shivering so."

He was conscious of the gathering chill, too. He suspected her shivering might also be from the frustration and uncertainty of the situation. He came to stand next to her, and tentatively held out his arm. "May I?"

She moved against his side, and he wrapped an arm around her shoulders. He knew she was small, at least several inches shorter than Lizzy or Isabella, but he hadn't quite appreciated the difference until his arm was around her.

He could not at first feel how cold she was, nor did she probably get any warmth from him. But as they stood there for another few minutes, he began to feel the coldness of her at his side and along his arm. She also sighed. Her body relaxed a little, though the shivering did not entirely stop. It reminded him of calming a frightened horse, trembling under his hands.

"Thank you," she said.

"You're welcome."

She looked toward the house. The top gables were visible from their angle. "If this is some sort of prank, I shall be very annoyed."

"Do you suspect the children?" he asked.

"Surely not, but possibly? No, I cannot believe this of them. Eleanor is a little minx and a lively girl, but she is not malicious or mean. Neither are the others."

"Then who was in your thoughts?"

"No one—I don't know."

He let her subside. Eventually, without saying anything, he curved his arm around and brought her to face him. She silently put her cold face against his chest, and he wrapped his other arm around her, protecting her from the growing bite of cold evening air.

Neither of them broke the silence. It seemed disrespectful to make her talk to him in such a vulnerable position. If she wanted to pretend that *he* was some sort of heated wall, that was her prerogative.

He felt her small body finally stop shivering in the circle of his embrace. There were not many women he had held this way. His mother, after the death of his father. His sister, when she'd been thrown from a horse, though thankfully not much hurt. No one like this; never a time that he'd wanted to stroke the hair at the nape of a woman's neck, or tilt her chin up that he might kiss her and warm up her cold lips.

The sunlight had left even the top of the wall now. Dusk came early in December, and already the shadows in the garden were becoming hard to decipher. It would be fully dark soon. He had to consciously freeze his hand to keep it from stroking up and down her back.

Perhaps Mary felt his aborted movement, for she chuckled. He could feel it in every part of himself, as if the chuckle had come from him. "If you had told me at the beginning of this trip that I would spend this long in your arms, I wouldn't have believed you."

"Ha—you would have slapped me, more like. And I would have deserved it."

"I don't usually slap people, even when they do deserve it. Perhaps I should make a start."

"Whoever did this has my vote."

"The Pemberley ghost."

They both chuckled and the combined movement made him take a sharp breath. They both began to speak at once.

His sudden, "Please forgive me," came at the same time as her, "Do you hear someone?"

"Sorry, what?" he said.

"Shush, listen."

They both listened, and then she shook her head, burying it against him again. "I was wrong. What did you say?

"I said, please forgive me for misjudging you."

She looked back up at him again. Her dark eyes held only muted light in the dusk. "In what way?"

"In possibly *every* way. I was rude to you on a number of occasions; I made baseless insinuations. You would have been truly justified in slapping me then. I allowed my judgement and understanding to be clouded by one misunderstanding and your, er—"

"Reputation?"

"Partially. I was also mislead by my own experiences as a child, but that is no excuse. I was wrong. My own observations as well as my brother's have given me proof of that, as well as your kindness to Georgiana, Eleanor, and Maggie. Not to mention your kindness in giving the main role back to Isabella; I almost forgot about that. You are a thoughtful person."

"Not really. I live for parties and friends and society; my reputation is not so far off."

"You needn't try so hard to hide your kindness. It's not a sin, even in the *beau monde*."

He felt her smile. "Maybe it is. You're too far on the fringes to know." She stiffened. "I didn't mean that as an insult—"

"It's fine. I am on the fringes; I accept it." As if his arm belonged to someone else, Fitz found his hand ghosting over her cheek. Her skin was so soft, so cold. "You should never be this cold."

"Don't ruin this," she said.

He dropped his hand.

"Everyone gets cold," she added. "Even wealth can't protect one from that, I've found."

Just then they both heard an upraised voice. "Miss Crawford? Colonel Fitzwilliam?"

Mary jerked away from him, and Fitz found his hands holding onto her waist, clutching her back instinctively. He forced his hands to drop again. What was the matter with him?

Still making eye contact, Mary raised her voice. "We're here! In the walled garden!"

"Coming, miss!" it sounded like one of the footmen. "What the devil, oh, excuse me... Somebody's rolled that barrel of tar in front of the door and chocked it with a wedge. Just a moment, miss, Colonel."

The footman successfully rolled the barrel away and wrenched the door open over the dirty snow and frozen mud. His curly black hair shone in the starlight and his breath puffed white in the air. "That was a bad trick! It's a good thing the little girl thought of you being outside."

Fitz frowned. "Did she? How helpful."

Mary shook her head and placed a hand on his arm. "Please don't say anything at present about the barrel."

"Are you sure, miss?" the footman asked. "It's a tall bit o'mischief if ever I've seen it."

"Yes, it is, but there will be a ruckus and... please refrain for now."

The footman looked to Fitz, and he concurred. "Whatever Miss Crawford wants. She is the principal victim."

"Nonsense. I have everything I could want. Let us go back at once."

{17}

THIS TIME THE ABSENCE of Colonel Fitzwilliam and Miss Crawford *had* been noted.

When it reached the children, after their early dinner at four o'clock, Maggie had rounded on Eleanor. "What did you *do*?"

"Nothing! I came up to the nursery with you to change our wet clothes like usual."

Maggie dragged her to the side. She was usually more gentle, but not today. "Did you lock them outside? It is very cold! We must tell someone at once. I told you that you were going too far."

"I didn't," Eleanor said. "I'm not a complete *ninny*. Perhaps they found a quiet room on their own."

Maggie loved her sister, but she did not believe her. She rushed down to the parlor, where more inquiries were being made.

"Have we checked the study, the lower gallery, or perhaps—the attic?" Lizzy asked. "They may each have gone their own way to find a quiet spot. With the theatrical tonight and the ball tomorrow, everything is at sixes and sevens. I'm certain there is no cause for alarm."

Maggie went quietly to her mother. "What if they are, er, trapped outside?"

"Outside?" her mother repeated. The assembled company all looked to the dark windows. The sun had gone down and there was only a little lingering light.

Mr. Darcy immediately dispatched several footmen to search the grounds around the house, and another to check the less-used rooms on the ground and first floors.

When Miss Crawford and Uncle Fitz came inside, cold and clearly tired, Maggie gave Eleanor a very harsh pinch.

"Ouch!"

"You deserve it."

There was much fawning over the two, and apologies from both Mr. and Mrs. Darcy. "I don't know how this could have happened," Lizzy added, "but if there's *anything* I can do to make it up to you, please tell me."

"It's a dashed odd house," put in Mr. Van Allen. "I don't accuse anyone, but I also don't scruple to say that I have *never* been so inconvenienced and yes, victimized in my life. Why, the ladder was knocked down when I was so obliging as to enter the attic for my wife and Miss Fitzwilliam. Then there was the statuette in front of the door; the dashed *locks* that keep changing. I was trapped in a storeroom for nigh on two hours! There's a ghost, I say, and any responsible host would *warn* their guests—"

Lizzy cut him off when she realized he would not stop. "We are dreadfully sorry, Mr. Van Allen—it is most strange and we are trying to make sure there are no miscommunications among the servants. But Mary, *anything* I can do for your comfort, please tell me. And of course, we can put off the theatrical—"

Isabella and Alicia both protested this. "Oh, no! Please do not. With the ball coming and most leaving the following day, it will never happen."

Colonel Fitzwilliam rubbed his cold hands together briskly. "I am happy to continue as planned, as long as I can get some coffee in the meantime. If Miss Crawford is feeling too exhausted, surely Mrs. Darcy or someone else could read for Don John."

Maggie glared at Eleanor. She could be careless, but this was bad even for her. Eleanor had not only jeopardized Uncle Fitz's and Miss Crawford's safety, she had jeopardized the play! Eleanor did not look nearly as sorry as she ought, but then that was *often* the way with Eleanor.

To Maggie's relief however, Miss Crawford seemed to be game. "I can do it, and some hot coffee would be delightful."

Mrs. Gardiner came up with her children to help them get into the "costumes" they had designed for themselves. For Maggie, it was one of her mother's plainer dresses, worn over her own frock, and double tucked at the waist with a sash to make it just reach the floor. Maggie did not wear long skirts yet, so she felt very grown up. There were some fake flowers that had been found in the attic, and a spray of these went in Maggie's hair, which her mother helped her to put up. "Just for tonight," she reminded her.

A similar arrangement had been made for Eleanor, though her dress was finer, as it had been borrowed from Miss Crawford. Mrs. Gardiner and Georgiana and Lizzy were all too tall for it to work, but Miss Crawford's dresses were shorter. It was a fine cerulean blue, and Maggie was a little jealous, if she was honest.

Their mother seemed to be helping them absently, with her thoughts elsewhere. After she helped the boys tie handkerchiefs around their small throats, adjust top hats borrowed from the gentlemen, and strap on makeshift scabbards, they were quite happy.

"Maggie, my dear, wait a moment." Her mother looked very serious as the younger three filed out of the room. "How did you know that Miss Crawford and Colonel Fitzwilliam were outside?"

Maggie dug the toe of her slipper into the pile of the fine carpet. "Well, it was logical, wasn't it? We hadn't seen them come in."

"But we were all sure they had done so. Maggie, tell me the truth."

"It was—it was Eleanor! I'm sorry. She hatched an idea to give the two of them more time together. We thought they might get married."

"More time together, as in...?" Her mother's eyes closed. "Oh, no. Don't tell me. She has been the one locking doors?"

"Once it was me." Maggie hung her head, though she could not help adding, "But mostly it was Eleanor! She has not told me every time, but she must have been doing it *far* too much based on the commotion she's caused."

"This is dreadful, particularly today. Miss Crawford could have been very ill." She pressed a hand to her head. "Miss Crawford will be furious. Rightly so! Your poor cousin Lizzy has been at her wit's end as her first house party teeters on the edge of disaster, and it was you two all along!"

"Do we have to tell her?" Maggie ventured.

Her mother gave her a stern look. "Yes, we must tell her. More importantly, you and your sister owe Miss Crawford a sincere apology."

"Do we have to tell Miss Crawford *tonight*?" Maggie swiped tears out of her eyes. "She will be angry, and everything will be ruined! Eleanor will be furious with me for telling; Uncle Fitz will probably never speak to us again." Maggie's gasps were changing rapidly to sobs. "I am so sorry, Mama!"

Her mother wrapped an arm around her. "I hope none of those things happen, but I cannot promise they will not. There are consequences when we do wrong; and it was wrong to play tricks and manipulate our friends."

"It wasn't my idea," Maggie said. "I promise."

"I believe you, and Eleanor will bear the brunt of our discipline. But you are almost twelve, Maggie, you are old enough to understand that this was not a good plan."

"I know."

Her mother squeezed her shoulders. "However, thinking it over, you may be right about not confessing the whole tonight. I would prefer to get it out in the open, but that would spoil everyone's pleasure. We will do it tomorrow morning."

Maggie nodded sadly. "I daresay I won't be able to enjoy it at all, with the shame of tomorrow hanging over my head. I suppose that is a just punishment for my involvement."

"It is, but I suspect you will still enjoy yourself. Now, let me help you tuck this dress in again, for it has slipped, and then you may go downstairs."

Before the play began, Mrs. Gardiner took her younger daughter aside. She did not relish the idea of ruining her daughter's evening, but this was a serious transgression. Mrs. Gardiner did not intend to tell her husband until the morrow, for although he was an excellent man and a good father, she suspected they might not see eye to eye on the current issue.

Mrs. Gardiner led her into the small drawing room. She was truly shocked at what her daughter had done. A few tricks was one thing, but to purposefully lock two people out of the house when there was snow on the ground! And not to speak of it even after darkness fell and the temperature dropped? Shocking.

"Mother, what is the matter? Are you angry?"

"I am not yet angry; I am stunned. Maggie told me everything concerning your plot with Miss Crawford and

Colonel Fitzwilliam. Eleanor! *How* could you think it right? I have been lenient with you in a way my mother was not, but I thought you understood—I thought there was more concern, more kindness and common sense in you than this. I am very disappointed."

"But it is out of kindness and concern that I acted! I truly like Miss Crawford and Uncle Fitz. You have told us how it can be difficult to become acquainted due to society's restrictions, and so I only sought to give them a little more time together."

"I said *that* in context of caution to you and Maggie. I meant that although you may feel that you know a gentleman well, it is prudent to make sure you know a man's true character before you venture in an engagement... I did not mean that a woman must somehow contrive to spend hours alone with a gentleman before marrying him. It is very improper!"

"I only did it twice, I promise! And they would have been alone anyway, in the ballroom, or in the library."

"It must have been far more than twice, based on the commotion and questions it has caused. I shall be devastated if you lie to me, Eleanor. That is even worse than the first."

"I am not lying, Mama. I did—also—roll up a carpet and lock a few other doors. But those did not constrain Miss Crawford in any way! Those times it was just to slow down Mr. Van Allen. And I did not do that very much."

Mrs. Gardiner had her own doubts about that situation. As a matter of fact, she had nudged a heavy statuette just an inch or two to the side, when she realized Mr. Van Allen was going to approach Miss Crawford while she practiced harp alone. Not that she had any intention of telling Eleanor that.

Mrs. Gardiner pressed on. "And the kitchen garden today? Was that to be more time together?"

"No. I told Maggie, and I will tell you, I did not do that."

Mrs. Gardiner studied her daughter carefully. Until today, she would have said that Eleanor was no liar. Today, her confidence was shaken, but there was not a particle of deception in Eleanor's eyes. "Very well, I believe you," she said. "But again, if I find you are deceiving me in some way I have not yet detected—that will be very terrible."

"Are you going to... tell everyone?"

"Not yet. You and Maggie may enjoy the play, but you will both confess and apologize to Colonel Fitzwilliam and Miss Crawford tomorrow. You also owe an apology to your cousin."

Eleanor was made of sterner stuff than Maggie. "Very well, I understand. But I will not apologize to Mr. Van Allen. I cannot. He is a very rude man, and Miss Crawford does not like him. He deserved to be inconvenienced, and I am not sorry for it."

Mrs. Gardiner compressed her lips. On her own observation, she had come to much the same conclusion about the unpleasantness of Mr. Van Allen and his pursuit of Miss Crawford—hence her small and uncharacteristic act of malice toward him. It would never do to encourage Eleanor in this, however. "Since he was not at the crux of your plan, we will not involve him. But absolutely no more tricks, Eleanor. None."

"Yes, Mother."

Mrs. Gardiner released her and rubbed her throbbing head. Lizzy and Jane had never given her this sort of trouble. She shuddered to think of Eleanor at seventeen. At least the child had excellent instincts, but heaven forbid she turn her mind to mischief. Maggie would be a docile, well-behaved young woman; Eleanor was different.

Mrs. Gardiner had long since realized that her daughters might have much higher prospects in husbands due to Lizzy and Jane's marriages to men of fortune. Mrs. Gardiner would be a very strange mother indeed if the thought had never crossed her mind. Not in a thousand worlds would she take advantage of Mr. Darcy or Mr. Bingley, but she did want them to think well of her children. Unfortunately, she felt sure Eleanor and Maggie had burnt their bridges with Mr. Darcy completely.

She sighed and crossed the hall. Tomorrow morning, they would all three take their lumps.

The play was a huge success, at least for most of the party assembled at Pemberley. It was an event that Lizzy, Georgiana, and Darcy would reference for many years to come. They remembered it rather better and more cohesively than everyone else, as the three of them did not have parts and could sit and watch at their leisure.

Harold was also a fixed part of the audience, along with his mother, though she dozed off at least once, and he snoozed through most of the fourth act. Three rows of chairs had been moved in front of the impromptu stage, and while the other players would sit there between their own scenes, watching the others, only those five were able to watch the entire production.

Georgiana had the pleasure of having her backdrop greatly appreciated, and Lizzy summed up most of their feelings when she said, "It is one thing to draw a small sketch or painting of a flower, but to paint something on such a large scale with depth and detail, with only the supplies you had available in the house—excellent work, Georgiana!"

The children were the most costumed, though Alicia and Isabella had managed to make two historical Italian ensembles—or at least that is what Lizzy supposed them to be attempting. They used several old petticoats found in the storage of Pemberley's attic, which gave them quite a different silhouette than their usual slim dresses. Whether they looked Italian or appropriate for Shakespeare's day, no one knew or cared.

Halfway through, Darcy leaned toward her. "I am surprised how many people have memorized their lines. It is not half bad."

"That is high praise indeed, from you," Lizzy said. "Perhaps we should make it a yearly tradition."

"Well, I don't know—"

"I'm teasing."

He nudged her with his elbow, and she leaned her head on his shoulder. Soon after this was an intermission which had been agreed beforehand to be a break for supper. Instead of several courses in the dining room, however, it was a simple buffet brought to the ballroom as soon as Lizzy rang the bell.

The meal was not nearly as extensive as the preparations for the ball the following day, but there were cold meats, sugar-glazed radishes, pickled vegetables, cream tarts, and plum cake. The plum cake was usually a breakfast food, but Lizzy had ordered it particularly as a treat for the children. There was also claret, wine, and hot spiced ginger beer for those who wished.

There was a general hubbub as the players and "audience" mingled and exchanged extravagant compliments. Lizzy always found it amusing in this sort of scenario, that whenever someone *gave* a compliment they felt they were being generous and exaggerated with their praise, but when they *received* a compliment, they glowed as if an editor for the London papers had given them an expert review. Such dual thinking was not new to her, but it was striking how one person could hold two contradictory ideas in their head at the same time.

At any rate, Lizzy passed out her compliments freely, balancing Darcy who was not adept at grandiose compliments. She tempered his "acceptable" and "better than expected," with "amazing presence" and "hilarious timing." She also accepted compliments to herself on behalf of the excellent cook that Darcy employed.

Everyone seemed to be having a good time, but Lizzy kept a watchful eye on Miss Crawford. The poor lady had had a difficult day and might become overtired. Then there was Mr. Van Allen's persecution of her. Lizzy and Darcy had discussed the situation the previous evening in his bedroom.

"If he was single," Lizzy said, "I would say he was dangling after Miss Crawford, but he is not! His poor wife is spectator to it all. It is the most disgusting thing I have ever seen."

He'd frowned. "I didn't observe this. I did notice the fellow dipping rather deep the last few nights. He wasn't dead drunk, but he was far from sober. Has he been inappropriate?"

"It is hard to say. I have not seen him passing the line. It is in small things. He is always leaning over to whisper in her ear, or placing a hand on her arm, or *watching* her. And in her response—oh, she is bright and bold and lively—but I can see that her flesh crawls at his proximity."

"Should I get rid of them? The roads are passable, if not good."

"I don't think so. It would cause such an outcry for the gain of only two days. I must confess, however, that I locked one of those doors." Lizzy bit her lip. "I suspected he was looking for her, and Mrs. Reynolds had just given me all the keys that were taken up. It was too easy, and I knew I would not be suspected as there has already been some trouble."

She'd thought Darcy might cut up rather stiff over it, but instead he only laughed silently. He kissed her forehead and stroked her cheek. "Thank you for the confession, but there are far worse things. I regret that I allowed him to trick me into an invitation, but I daresay his bad manners excuse any slight lapse in ours." He frowned. "I do wonder what in the blazes happened in all those other instances. Pemberley does *not* have a ghost."

{18}

During intermission, Mr. Van Allen ate five candied radishes in a row with his eyes fixed on Miss Crawford. If he hadn't borne the brunt of continual mishaps at Pemberley, he would not have believed her excuse about being "locked in a garden."

He still was not sure he believed it. He knew what people who were "locked in gardens" did. He resented that Mary would dally with Colonel Fitzwilliam while giving him nothing but a cold shoulder. The more he watched them, the more convinced he became.

Mary looked at the colonel more. He looked at her more. And it was not just looking. There was a possessiveness to the colonel's actions. It was in the way he oriented around her, in a new sort of intentness to his look, in a sort of hunger that had his hands always half-reaching for her.

Mr. Van Allen took his plate to stand next to his own wife, but she ignored him. She chattered with Isabella, and only really looked at him when he eventually cleared his throat.

"You did very well as Hero, my dear. Quite the beautiful heroine."

Alicia's eyes lit up at his praise, but he didn't see it because he was looking to see if Mary noticed his attention to his wife. She hadn't. The colonel was standing near her, laughing, and only Van Allen caught the way his hand moved toward her waist, only to be drawn back and tucked behind him in military fashion.

Yes, something had happened. That little *trollop.*

Colonel Fitzwilliam could not help himself. He'd long liked Miss Crawford, and now that he did not have the excuse of thinking her a flirt or worse, he could not stay away. At least half of his stubborn persistence in thinking the worst of her must have been a protection for himself. While he thought badly of her character, he did not have to seriously consider his own feelings.

Now he admitted that ever since the Seftons' ball, he had been determined to think the worst. He had begun to fall in love with her, only to feel deep disappointment when Van Allen and she—as he thought—openly flirted with one another.

Every day after that, he had avoided his own disappointment by categorizing her as a relentless flirt.

Fitz drank claret during the intermission meal, and with every intention in the world of behaving, his hands had a mind of their own. It was all he could do not to warm her hands in his, not to press her arm in support, not to wrap his arm around her waist when she stood next to him.

It felt natural; why should he have to stand next to her and *not* touch her? What a ridiculous thing. There was an innate magnetism to Miss Crawford, and he had finally and fully succumbed to it.

He relinquished his cup to the buffet table and forced himself into parade rest. That seemed to the only position, long drilled into him, which stilled his questing hands.

What had she meant when she told him not to "ruin" it? He ought not to have touched her face in the garden, that was his fault, but did she dislike the setting, or did she dislike *him*? He did not want to think that, nor did her manner now indicate it, but he could not be sure.

While in the dark and cold, he had thought of little but kissing her, of wrapping more fully around her shivering form. Was she merely thinking what a great, stupid oaf he was? It was painful to recognize his desires only to know that rejection was still likely.

Regardless, Fitz had no intention of letting Van Allen near her tonight. She would not be annoyed. Fitz seemed to be in good company in this desire; every time the man came their direction, someone cut him off with questions or compliments. Fitz never even had to intervene.

The play resumed, and Fitz played his part with what gusto he could. It *was* rather fun to spar with his sister Isabella, who was clearly having the time of her life, though he could not help feeling that it would have been thrilling to play against Miss Crawford.

During the second half of the play, Miss Crawford had far less of a role. Don John ran off before the end of the play, so she was able to sit in the audience for almost the entire last hour.

He caught her eye rather often as he recited his lines, but that was not his fault. Who else was he to look at? Harold? Darcy?

Not likely.

The second half of the play was more enjoyable for Mary than the first. She was fully warm now, filled with good food, and feeling more benign towards everybody.

This was partly because she'd seen Mr. Van Allen spend a solid quarter of an hour with Alicia during the intermission, which was an excellent development. It was also partly because she could sit at her leisure and watch instead of springing up every quarter of an hour to give what could only be described as a tolerable performance as the villain of the piece.

To be sure, she had rather relished some of Don John's speeches. "I cannot hide what I am: I must be sad when I have cause and smile at no man's jests, eat when I have stomach and wait for no man's leisure, sleep when I am drowsy and tend on no man's business, laugh when I am merry and claw no man in his humor."

It was not true of Mary, but she rather wished it was. She often smiled when she was in a rage, played merry when she was sad, and ate when she had no stomach. Shakespeare understood that only a villain dared to live as they felt.

In any event, her role was done for the rest of the play, and she enjoyed watching Harry Hawksley claim his Hero, as well as the dashing and witty Benedick win his Beatrice.

After their secret love poetry was revealed within the play, Colonel Fitzwilliam dropped to one knee dramatically and took his sister's hand. "A miracle! Here's our own hands against our hearts. Come, I will have thee; but, by this light, I take thee for pity."

Isabella snorted and raised her proud chin, turning half away. "I would not deny you; but, by this good day, I yield upon great persuasion; and partly to save your life, for I was told you were in a consumption.

Fitz pulled her back toward him as he stood. "Peace! I will stop you there..."

The original line was, "I will stop your mouth." It was presumed Shakespeare choregraphed a bawdy kiss there, but Fitz only put one hand over her mouth, as a brother might, and lightly kissed her forehead.

The audience, which was now quite large as most of the roles were finished, laughed and clapped. The children were just as rapt and enthusiastic as if they were at the finest theater in the West End.

The final scene played out, and Mr. Holbrook, who had scarcely been able to sit during the entire length of the play, came in as the messenger. "My lord, your brother

John is taken in flight, and brought with armed men back to Messina."

Colonel Fitzwilliam looked momentarily grave. "Think not on him till to-morrow: I'll devise thee brave punishments for him. Strike up, pipers!"

For "pipers," Bertie played a tin whistle with moderate skill and great enthusiasm. Fitz and Isabella, as well as Harry and Alicia, who were playing the other lovesick couple, did a small section of a country dance. They formed a square and did the two steps that brought them forward and backward, and then Fitz and Isabella—rather taller than Harry and Alicia—made an arch with their arms that the other couple skipped through.

Bertie stopped on a long, trilled note, and the final players held hands and bowed.

Behind them, looking tired but pleased, was Mr. Holbrook, and next to him, looking bored and *not* pleased, was Mr. Van Allen, who had also been in the last scene.

Everyone rose and clapped again. Fitz produced a small posey of flowers for his sister. It was composed of a few of the hardy white flowers they'd noticed against the wall in the kitchen garden. He must have run back to collect them or tasked a footman to do so. It was thoughtful and kind.

Isabella grinned and tucked them in her sash. "Thank you, Fitz!"

Mary felt warm just from watching their interaction. She had heard once that you could safely judge a man on how he treated his mother. She wondered if the same held true for sisters. If so, Colonel Fitzwilliam would pass with flying colors.

Of course, she counted *her* brother as intensely loyal, but that had not stopped him from betraying Fanny by running off with Maria. Perhaps there was no way to tell what a gentleman would be like in love, unless one... loved them.

She shook her head. She was getting far ahead of herself, but the phantom feeling of Colonel Fitzwilliam's arms, warm and strong, was hard to shake. As was his unquestioning respect for her wishes.

Lizzy gave instructions for the servants to finish preparing the ballroom the following morning and led them all back to the drawing room. Mr. and Mrs. Knightley excused themselves, and Mrs. Gardiner took the children off to bed at once, but the rest joined in a second celebration of their efforts.

Somehow Mary did not have to contend with Van at all. Perhaps he was either too petulant or too prideful to continue harassing her. She would accept either with thankfulness.

Alicia seemed to be in a brittle mood and flirted boldly with Mr. Hawksley, so Mary avoided her gaze, but otherwise enjoyed herself. Colonel Fitzwilliam stayed nearby, and his easy smile and happy ways were once again hers.

Reluctantly, Mary admitted that she was relieved to have his approbation again. As much as she did not want to care, apparently his good opinion mattered to her. Stupid female emotions! Truly, she could not subdue a giddy feeling of joy that he no longer thought badly of her.

"Your tea, Miss Crawford." He offered it to her after going to Lizzy's small circle to retrieve a cup for her. "One sugar, no milk."

"Perfect, thank you."

"I hope you're quite comfortable; not overly tired or chilled?"

"I'm not such a poor creature, though I shall not mind the two hot bricks that Mrs. Darcy's good servants bring up each night."

Fitz looked a little flushed. "Yes, a luxury indeed."

"Though everyone has already said so, allow me to congratulate you on a fine performance."

"Thank you, it was certainly diverting." He lowered his voice. "I daresay you noticed, but Maggie and Eleanor were rather subdued."

"I did notice."

"Do you wish me to speak with Mr. or Mrs. Gardiner? If the tar barrel was a trick they played, they must be chastised."

"Let us leave it for now. I am still dubious as to their guilt."

"As you wish." His hand briefly covered hers before he snatched it away again. The faintest impression of warmth remained. "I'm going to retire; I'm surprisingly tired myself. Goodnight, Miss Crawford."

"Goodnight."

{ 19 }

MARY'S MAID HELPED HER GET READY for bed, undoing the string of buttons on the side of her forest green dress, and pressing it after helping Mary slip out of it.

She also helped Mary undo the pins and pearls in her hair, and brushed her short curls vigorously before Mary put on a cap. Her hair was a little longer than her shoulders. She ought to have it cut again soon. The fashionable "crop" suited Mary's small face and made it easier to put up in the back.

She washed her face and blotted it gently with a cloth, for it was a little chill-burned and she did not want to redden and irritate her skin.

Then it was off with her petticoats, and quickly into her nightdress and the dressing gown. The two hot bricks had been delivered; the counterpane turned down. She got into bed quickly, pulling the blankets up to her neck. The warmth around her feet was heavenly. Bless Pemberley and its luxuries.

Her maid shook the dress out vigorously and hung it in the wardrobe. Mary's deep gold ball gown had also been unfolded and hung there, allowing it to air out prior to the ball.

After dousing the lamp and leaving a lit candle next to Miss Crawford's bed, the maid dumped the basin water back into the pitcher to take away with her. She checked that the chamber pot was in easy reach under the edge of the bed, and then took her leave.

Finally alone, Mary blew out the candle and pulled the covers over her head, quite as a child might. She pressed cool hands to her wind-reddened cheeks and rubbed her stocking-clad feet over the warm part of the bed.

She felt a fizzy sort of excitement, a strange anticipation she had not felt for a long time. Was it possible that she was falling in love with Colonel Fitzwilliam? And would she allow it of herself?

Mary lay awake for some time. She could not pretend that her thoughts were purely analytical. Nor did she devote much time to the culprit behind the incident. She had her suspicions, but it wouldn't do any good to canvas them now. She would be leaving Pemberley the day after tomorrow anyway.

No, Mary felt more than she thought. She was just as female as anyone, and the thrill of the garden must be gone through multiple times. She almost wished it had ended differently, but in the moment, she'd felt that it was perfect. Being held by a man, protected, appreciated—without taint from her ambition or morality or his doubts or impulses—she had not wanted that moment to be destroyed.

In retrospect, she realized he might have thought it a comprehensive rejection, but she could clear that up in a trice.

If she wanted to.

Did she? Mary fell asleep wondering.

Her face was free of the blanket when she awoke, though her feet were tangled. It was almost pitch dark in her room, for only a little moonlight came in around the dark drapes at the window. She rubbed her eyes sleepily. Was it the maid, Sarah, laying the fire just before dawn? Perhaps it was one of the children? Had Mary slept that long?

She heard quiet footsteps.

"Eleanor, is that you?" she asked. "If you've come to apologize—"

A dark gray shape separated from the darkness in a few hasty steps. It was much larger person than Eleanor. His weight was suddenly on the blanket and a hand pressed against her face, pushing her down into the feather pillow.

She was stifled. Her gasp, her shock, her thoughts all stifled. The air whistled in and out of her nose. He was half sitting on her arm.

"Be quiet." Mr. Van Allen whispered. "Or someone will hear us."

As his hand moved, she sucked in a breath. When she didn't scream, he moved his hand. "That's better."

"This is ridiculous; you must be drunk." Despite herself, Mary's voice was quiet. "Get out. Go back to Alicia."

"Tried that. I came to *my* wife, as is *my* right, and all she would say was that I hardly looked at her tonight. She said she tried to make me jealous by flirting with young Hawksley, and that I didn't care. She was right. I didn't. You used Colonel Fitzwilliam as your foil, trying to make me jealous, didn't you? You women are all alike, only *you* happened to succeed; aren't you clever?" He was all but on top of her, one hand pinning her shoulder down, the other hovering over her mouth. The layers between them didn't mute the heat of his body.

Mary was not scared, or not very, she was mostly angry. "You idiot, Van. Will you involve us both in a stupid and embarrassing scandal? Stop making speeches and get off me this instant." She wriggled to the side, but the blankets were tight, and he must be partially on her nightdress as well. "I am no barque of frailty or Bird of Paradise for you to treat me like this."

He scoffed. "You haven't any father or much of a brother to protect you though, have you? I daresay your uncle would not be surprised; he knows your reputation as well as anyone."

"Don't make a further fool of yourself. You'll regret this in the morning. Go away at once and I won't say anything."

Suddenly he kissed her. Mary did not expect it, and she was confirmed that—if not drunk—he had dipped rather deep. Wrestling one arm out from under the constricting blanket, she slapped him.

He grabbed her wrist.

Mary stilled. "I'll scream. I'll wake the house. I may have played your game quietly, but not anymore. You know I can be loud when needed." Her eyes had adjusted to the dim light, and she could just make out the jut of his nose, the wetness on his lips, and the line of moonlight reflected in his eyes.

"Who will believe you? You're already ruined because I'm here. No one here cares about you, why would they believe you innocent? Not if I speak against you."

Mary felt a little of her strength melt away. Colonel Fitzwilliam and Lord Matlock would believe her, she was almost sure. Everyone else—well, the idiot was probably right. Lizzy and Emma liked her, but they did not know her. They were so happy in their loving, committed marriages—what tolerance did they have for scandal and mess? As for their husbands, no. The worthy Mr. and Mrs. Gardiner? Everyone knew the middle class had very high moral standards. They would condemn her for Van's presence in her room; no further proof necessary. Mr. Holbrook and Mr. Hawksley—she shuddered at the mere idea of their involvement in this situation; they were mere boys.

"You agree, don't you?" he said. "You're among strangers, my dear. Are *you* going to cause that 'stupid and embarrassing scandal' you spoke of?"

It was just like him to turn her words against her.

Mary took a shallow breath and screamed.

It was not as easy as she expected to suddenly mimic a heroine from a Gothic romance, but she startled Van enough that he jumped rather badly. She got off another yelp before his hand was back over her mouth.

He'd jumped so badly, however, that she had managed to slide away from him. She bit and flailed and tumbled ungracefully to the floor on the far side of her bed.

Her elbow and knee hit the ground first, painfully, barely cushioned by the thin rug that stretched from the bed to the window.

"Sarah! Becky! Clara!" She called the names of the maids she knew. Even in this situation, she couldn't help but think that perhaps scandal could be avoided.

Van cursed and backed away from the bed.

Mary pulled the drapes back from the window, welcoming the cold that radiated from the glass panes along with the moonlight that lit the room.

Van was almost to the hall door when a sharp knock was followed immediately by Lizzy opening the door and entering. "What is wrong, Miss Crawford? We heard a commotion—"

She broke off, mouth ajar at the surprise of finding Mr. Van Allen in the room.

The maid, Sarah, was next. "Did you call me, miss?"

Mary was just thinking that perhaps she could avert disaster and speak only to these two. That would not be so bad as she'd feared.

Then the gentlemen started to appear, along with Isabella, Emma, Georgiana, and Lady Matlock. The hall beyond the maid seemed to be flooding with persons. Perhaps Mary had screamed louder than she thought. They were all illuminated by a lamp held by Mr. Darcy, and another by Lady Matlock, both of whom had apparently kept their heads long enough to think of bringing a light. The ladies were wrapped in various fine dressing gowns, like a pastel chorus from a Greek tragedy, all lavender and pink.

Mr. Darcy shone the lamp over Sarah's shoulder. "Move, Sarah, be quick." The maid ducked out of the way, and Mr. Darcy came in next to his wife. "What has happened? Is someone ill?"

Lizzy's eyes snapped with anger. "I do not think so."

Mr. Van Allen shook his head. "I don't know, I thought I heard something as well. Came to check on Mary."

He had turned to face her as well, becoming one of the tableau that surrounded Mary. She was as isolated as if she were alone on a stage.

She had another decision to make, fiends seize it. If she allowed Van to claim that he only came in response to her cry, it would avert scandal. She could blame it on a nightmare or some other folly. But it would embolden him, the wretched man.

"Is that right, Mary?" Lizzy asked. "You are quite pale. Perhaps we ought to clear the room—" Lizzy gestured sharply, indicating that Mr. Van Allen ought to leave.

That was when Colonel Fitzwilliam edged into the doorway past the pastel watchers.

His face was set in harsh lines as he took in the characters of the impromptu play. Before Mary could cudgel her brain to make yet another decision, Fitz turned and planted a flush hit on Mr. Van Allen. Van staggered backward and hit the bed.

Fitz's hand clenched around the collar of his night shirt and hauled him up. Then he hit him again. This time Van dropped completely, crumpling in a large heap with his head nearly under the bed.

"Stop—*stop*." said Mr. Darcy. "You may be in the right of it, but no more. Not here." He put a firm hand on his cousin's arm.

Mary had kept quite a remarkable hold on her spirits, but ever since she screamed, her mental perturbation was immense. The scene now was almost too much for her, strong as she was. She gasped and felt nearly faint as she saw Van's nose dripping blood on the patterned rug.

"Do come out, Miss Crawford," Lizzy said. "You are perfectly safe. Darcy, please get rid of all these people."

Mary looked at the assembled faces, both those in the room and those craning their necks to see from the hall, and she felt anything but safe, even as Mr. Darcy began to corral some back to their rooms.

Colonel Fitzwilliam understood what had happened, as she'd hoped he would, but there were so many other people present! So many people to spread terrible rumors, to condemn her.

"I know it looks dreadful. Him being here." Mary somehow couldn't bring herself to come around the bed. The furniture was protection of a flimsy sort. "I assure you it isn't as bad as it seems. Despite what you may have heard of my reputation—You see, I could not lock my door—"

Lizzy furrowed her brow. "Dear Mary, we aren't accusing you of anything. We've all seen how things lie; we're only concerned for you. What do you mean you could not lock your door?"

"You took up the keys several days ago. You had the housekeeper collect them to prevent any more mischief. Didn't you?"

"Not any of the bedroom keys," Lizzy said.

"Oh. When mine disappeared, I thought it was that."

Colonel Fitzwilliam flexed his hand. His knuckles were red in the light of the two lamps. He used a foot to shove Van Allen onto his back, then searched his pockets. He brought a key out of the left one. "Is this it?"

"Yes," Mary said faintly. She could hardly believe her luck. "Then you all believe me? That this wasn't..."

"My dear girl," said Mrs. Gardiner briskly. "We all know what sort of scoundrel that man was—we all saw how he persecuted you! You've no need to worry at present." She came around the bed to Mary and righted her dressing gown. She wrapped it more firmly around her slim waist and tied the sash again. "That's right, my dear. Let's go to—to Lizzy's sitting room while the men deal with *him*. It is just down the hall, next to her bedroom. Perhaps she can rouse the servants for a bit of tea."

Mr. Knightley wadded a handkerchief under the man's bleeding nose. "Just as well not to sully the carpet further," he said, with great disregard for the rich, unconscious gentleman at his feet. "Don't worry, Miss Crawford."

Everyone seemed to believe in her innocence even without the proof. Their air of comfort and kindness was rather a shock. She would have been less surprised if there had been harsh tones and at least a *few* harsh questions. Her ignorance of the sort of people she'd fallen in with had deceived her.

With many calm words and gentle urging, Mrs. Gardiner herded Mary out of the room and down the hall to Lizzy's small sitting room.

By now Mr. Darcy had got rid of most of the onlookers, though Mary saw Isabella peering out a slightly-opened door, and it looked like Mr. Gardiner and Mr. Knightley were going to help Colonel Fitzwilliam carry Van out of her room.

The door to Lizzy's sitting room closed behind her, and Mary found herself with only the two ladies: Lizzy and Mrs. Gardiner. That was a bit of a relief. She was helped to a chair as if she was an invalid.

Mrs. Gardiner put a heavy wool blanket over her legs. "There we go. We will wait for tea here."

"Thank you," Mary said. "You are very kind. You mustn't think I'm going to faint or go into hysterics. I never do."

"We wouldn't blame you if you did, but that is probably for the best. In my experience, the aftermath of fainting is a sad disorientation and nausea."

Mary smiled faintly. "Hopefully both can be avoided. I'm perfectly clear-headed, just a little shaken."

Lizzy gripped her hands together. "I am so sorry, Miss Crawford. My husband and I have been regretting our invitation to that man almost since the minute it was given. If we had dreamed that he would dare insult a guest like this—we would have sent him packing."

"I was shocked myself," Mary admitted. "He must have been drunk, although he spoke coherently. He had argued with Alicia."

"That is no reason to attack a woman in her bedchamber. He is far worse than I thought," Mrs. Gardiner said.

Mary relaxed in her chair. "Yes, but least said, soonest mended. As long as he does not bother me again, I'd just as soon forget about this. Of course, with Mr. Hawksley and Mr. Holbrook in the house, plus Alicia herself, it will be impossible to control the rumors." Mary sighed and rubbed her aching head. "Perhaps you might ask Mr. Darcy to speak with them."

"I will do so," Lizzy said, "but you don't need think about rumors and ramifications yet. It matters more how *you* are doing."

Mary laughed. "You only think so because you are new to the limelight. Rumors are part of the fabric of my existence; I must care about them at all times."

"I believe what my niece means, is that—in short, Miss Crawford, how badly were you hurt? Should we call a doctor?"

"Heavens, no! Do not involve a doctor. I sustained a few bruises when I fell," she gestured to her knee and elbow, "but nothing worse happened."

"Your neck and shoulder looked rather red," Lizzy said.

Mary moved her dressing gown and saw that Van's grip had left some light bruises. "It's slight. They'll be gone in a few days."

"Is there some reason you feel you must make light of this?" Mrs. Gardiner asked. "My brother is a barrister, and I believe you could charge Mr. Van Allen with assault. It is only a misdemeanor, sadly, but some form of justice—"

"No, thank you. I appreciate your kindness, truly I do, but I must be the best judge of my next path."

Neither of them could argue with that.

"I've already received an invitation from my friend Lady Stornaway," Mary added, "and I will go to her house on my return to London. I only desire to avoid comment on this regrettable... event."

{ 20 }

FITZ POSITIONED HIMSELF NEAR the feet of the downed man to help carry him. "But where should we take him? We can hardly throw him in the room next to his poor wife."

Mr. Knightley twisted his lips. "Out the front door, belike."

Fitz laughed harshly, still fingering the key the blackguard had stolen. "I will if you will."

Mr. Knightley squatted next to Van Allen. "There must be an unused servant's room, or perhaps a cellar where he may be locked until he rouses. He must be spoken to when he awakes, and—depending on events—interrogated by an officer. I am a magistrate in Highbury, and I would want to be alerted in similar circumstances."

"A magistrate, I hadn't thought of that. Fitz clenched his fists as he thought of Miss Crawford's stricken yet resigned look. "Here's Darcy again."

When Darcy understood the question, he nodded. "Yes, there's a room. Not precisely a jail, more of a cupboard, but we can post one of the footmen to alert us when he wakes up."

Before ever they could hoist him up, Van Allen began to come around. Darcy put a restraining hand on Fitz's arm again. "Don't act rashly."

Van Allen sat up and grunted. He spat on the ground, blood and spit, and Darcy made a face. Mr. Knightley retrieved his handkerchief and handed it to Van Allen. "You'll use this, if you have the urge to be disgusting."

"What the devil..." Van wiped his bloody nose on the handkerchief. "You drew my cork, man."

They waited while he shook his head and got his bearings. Finally he braced himself against the bed frame and pushed himself up. The others stood with him.

Darcy gestured down the hall. "Come along with us; we need to speak."

Van Allen was a bit belligerent, inclined to go back to his guest room, but his head was aching and less than perfectly clear. When Darcy gestured into his study, Van slumped in. Darcy poured a small measure of brandy for him. "For your head."

"That's more like. Your Friday-faces are bad enough." He raised the tumbler to Colonel Fitzwilliam. "I'll even admit you got a fair hit in. Between gentlemen, I shan't hold a grudge."

Darcy feared for Fitz's teeth, his jaw was locked so tight.

"Perhaps you'll excuse us," Darcy told him. "Knightley and I can do what needs to be done. Mr. Gardiner also offered his services." Darcy was upset, but Fitz looked dangerously incensed. If he didn't get some distance, Darcy might end up fetching the magistrate for a case of manslaughter.

"I'd better." Fitz stalked out, and Darcy was relieved he was smart enough to do so.

Knightley took over. "Now, I'm a magistrate," he said to Van, "and I know the law. What you did could easily be considered assault with intent to rape."

Darcy's eyes widened, but Knightley was stoic as he continued. "I daresay you don't think it would stick, but recollect that Miss Crawford is a woman of quality. We have a whole household willing to corroborate that she did not encourage you."

Van laughed, using the dirty handkerchief to wipe a fresh trickle of blood from his nose. "She's encouraged me many times in the past five years, publicly. And who's to say what my intent was? Or that she didn't invite me to her room herself?" He seemed to recollect himself. "Which she did. Don't know why she suddenly took a fuss."

Darcy's lip curled. The man's bold impudence was astounding.

Knightley only shook his head. "Lie to me if you want, but it won't fly. I've half a mind to fetch the local magistrate at once. Darcy's word carries clout in Derbyshire, you know. The magistrate could detain you until he does a full investigation."

"That's absurd. I'm a man of fortune, I can't be kept against my will on such a small charge."

"You stole her key; this is a serious matter. On the word of Mr. Darcy, as the master of Pemberley, and myself, as a magistrate and gentleman of quite a few more years than yourself, I think the local magistrate would detain you."

Knightley's unshakeable poise was getting to Mr. Van Allen.

"The devil he would... What are you saying?"

"If you do not immediately cease to persecute Miss Crawford, and if you dare to whisper a word of calumny against her; you will regret it." Even this was not said in a tone of threat, but calm certainty.

Van Allen's chin still jutted out, but his swallow was visible. "A lot of fuss over nothing. Didn't know you were a magistrate, but I should've guessed. The most boring gentleman I've ever met."

"Thank you."

"I haven't any desire to speak of Miss Crawford. She's been a terrible tease; she's a light-skirt in fine gowns, that's what."

"Such things as that are exactly what you will not say."

"Oh, fiend seize you, I will not say it. I'll leave as planned after the ball, a model of propriety."

"That ship, as they say, has sailed. You'll leave in the morning. If Mrs. Van Allen wishes to stay, we will contrive to convey her home when she wishes."

"Leaving before the ball? Won't that cause comment?"

Darcy spoke up. "Less than if Fitz breaks your face, which he is precious close to doing. You've told us boxing is in your line, but he once went seventeen rounds with Gentleman Jackson."

Between the threat of both the law and the fist, Van Allen was at last subdued. There were no spare guest rooms, but they tucked him up in one of the maid's rooms and moved her to the housekeeper's parlor for the rest of the night. Van put up a bit of fuss about that, but both men were serious about not inflicting him on his wife in his current frustration.

As they left him there, with a footman yawning sleepily outside the room, Darcy frowned.

He held the light for them as they traversed back up the dark stairwell. It was the servants' stair, and rather steep.

At the top, he asked, "Is this best? I can hardly stand to let a villain leave my house like that. His attack was brazen."

"I abhor it as you do, but there is very little we can do. It is true the law is not on Miss Crawford's side. Even were she to win such a suit, which is not at all certain, to the eyes of most in polite society she would be ruined. This can't be unknown to you."

"It is not, and yet, I am shocked. To think of such an event with Elizabeth, or with Emma—surely you cannot be so resigned."

"I try not to say so often, but I do have more experience than you. Females, particularly ones without fortune, are sadly at risk. That is partially why I was so glad to see Emma's friend Harriet safely married to a good man. She is just the sort the law would not even pretend to protect. Supposedly Miss Crawford should be, but even then the laws fall short."

Mary sipped a cup of tea as the downstairs clock struck two loud gongs. "Is it only two? It feels like it should be much later. You should both seek your rest soon. Mrs. Gardiner, you have your children to care for, and Lizzy, you still have a ball tomorrow!"

"I suppose I do," said Lizzy. "I cannot very well cancel; word would not reach all the guests in time. You certainly do not need to attend if you don't wish. I can have a cozy dinner brought up to you."

"Perhaps I should pretend to be prostrate to prove my sensibility, but I would much prefer a ball! I enjoy balls, you know, and too much solitary time would not be my first choice. You must let me know if I can be of help tomorrow. I hosted many at my uncle's house, and I would be happy to be your *aide-de-camp*, if you would like."

"Thank you, that would be lovely. Hopefully the doors will cooperate, and we will not have more than the usual vexation of fallen puddings and underdone sweetmeats."

Mrs. Gardiner cleared her throat. "As to that, I'm afraid I have a mortifying confession to make. It appears that Eleanor, and to some extent Maggie, have been on a bit of a campaign. They have been attempting to arrange the party as they like, and they have been responsible for the mishaps and mysteries for the last ten days." It was clear Mrs. Gardiner was laboring under very deep chagrin. "How they came to such a bold and naughty plan and carried it out, I do not know. I am shocked. I deeply apologize. If they had not done this, there never would have been the confusion about the keys. Eleanor and Maggie are going to give their own apologies in the morning."

Lizzy stared at her. "Surely not! Eleanor and Maggie are so sweet! A silly trick now and again, yes, but what could be their motive for this? They wouldn't make a plan simply to anger and annoy the guests; I cannot believe that."

Mrs. Gardiner stood, too distressed to sit. "The long and short of it is that they have been playing matchmaker. They wished to see Miss Crawford with Colonel Fitzwilliam—*very* naughty of them, and so I have told them. I hope—are you laughing, Miss Crawford?"

"Yes, I am." Mary wiped tears from her eyes. "I suspected it from the beginning, but I never caught them at it! And I was only the victim half the time—less than half the time. That made me pause."

"The other half of their little plot was to prevent Mr. Van Allen from intruding his presence on you."

"Which, given this evening, shows a rather keen insight on their part," Mary said. "I did not take him seriously. Oh, and the ladder! Mr. Van Allen was incensed to be trapped in the attic."

"Eleanor did not mention the ladder," Mrs. Gardiner said conscientiously. "But I wish *I* had taken her more seriously when she said that he had grabbed your wrist! It bothered her, and although I could not like it, I did not see precisely what I could do."

"Nor anyone, please do not lay blame on yourself. And do *not* tell Eleanor and Maggie the mischief caused with the keys. They don't deserve that. Please promise me you won't."

Mrs. Gardiner promised, both guilty and relieved.

When they had finished their tea, Mary excused herself and Mrs. Gardiner walked her back to her room. Mary was half-surprised not to see Colonel Fitzwilliam waiting in the hall. She'd expected he would want to check on her well-being. She wasn't sure if manners dictated that one thank a person for coming to blows in their defense, but it felt appropriate.

He was not there, however. The rug in her room had a wet spot where a housemaid had already been busy soaking and scrubbing the blood away. Mary's bed had been vigorously righted from the tangled mess it had been before. The bricks had been reheated.

"Would you like me to stay?" asked Mrs. Gardiner. "I am not quite old enough to be your mother's age, but I am not so far off either. I would not mind at all."

"No, thank you. I shall do very well."

Mrs. Gardiner reluctantly left her alone.

Colonel Fitzwilliam had gone on an undirected, fast-paced walk of the house to work off his rage and frustration.

When he had calmed, he racked the balls in the billiard room and played a blistering game against himself. The fact he didn't shatter a cue was not for lack of trying.

When he heard Mrs. Gardiner escorting Mary back to her room, he waited. Everything in him wanted to comfort her. He needed to assure himself that she was not injured, and to assess how upset she was. If he knew anything of Mary, she was protesting that she was perfectly fine and that she had nothing in life but good things!

Fitz had grown up with a stern but concerned father, a loving mother, and two siblings who would do anything for him, in their own way. Compared to him, her life seemed severely lacking. Who could she look to with unquestioning confidence? Who were her protectors? Who was loyal to her no matter what?

She had truly thought the entire house full of people would find a man attacking her in her room and blame her for it. In looking back, Fitz felt even more guilt that she'd had to tell him not to touch her face in the garden. Was she always subjected to such liberties? Not as bad as tonight, surely, but it must be a motif.

Unfortunately, it was not his right to comfort her, and certainly not his role to interrogate her.

When Mrs. Gardiner came back into the hall, he stepped out of the room and raised a hand to acknowledge her. She redirected her steps to the billiard room just as Darcy and Mr. Knightley were also returning from their talk.

The four convened in the billiard room, and it was an odd tableau. There was kind, middle-aged Mrs. Gardiner in her night-rail and dressing gown, Darcy looking precise to a pin, and himself, with only a hastily thrown on coat over his nightshirt.

Mr. Darcy nodded to Mrs. Gardiner. "Please thank your husband for his offer of legal advice. I think we will not need to pursue it."

"Not pursue it? Do we not agree what happened?" Fitz was still angry, but as Darcy and Knightley explained, he admitted that his knowledge of society backed up their decision. Mrs. Gardiner gave her approbation as well, though they all sat silently in shared disappointment and consternation that there was not more to do.

Then Mrs. Gardiner made a clean breast of the situation with her daughters.

"He grabbed her wrist?" Fitz asked.

"Apparently so. From what Miss Crawford let fall, I gather she thought if she rode the week out, the problem would be solved when the party broke up. Nor is she, I suspect, much in the company of those old enough or wise enough to show maturity and compassion. Generally she is at these sort of things with a rather fast set."

Darcy sighed. "So Lizzy was right that she asked to visit Pemberley in an effort to get away from a sordid or difficult situation." He half-smiled. "Lizzy is generally right."

There was not much else to be said, and they broke apart to take what rest they could.

Fitz found when he'd gone to his room that he still had Mary's key in his hand. He'd bruised his palm with how tensely he clutched it.

{21}

THE NEXT MORNING, MARY WAS WARNED not to come down right away. She was kindly told that they would send a note when Mr. Van Allen was gone, but Mary had never followed directions she disliked.

Perhaps it was not the purest impulse, but she wanted to show a bold face before Van left. Her pride demanded that his last glimpse of her be on *her* terms, not his.

This was all well and good, but she had forgotten Alicia. Mary didn't even make it to the front hall before Alicia made a scene.

Alicia was following a footman down the broad front stairs, but she turned back when she saw Mary out of the corner of her eye. Her large brown eyes were red from weeping, but there was still a snap to them. It was that lively edge to her gaze that had made Alicia the *nonpareil* of the previous crop of debutantes. Today her gaze snapped from temper, not coquetry.

"How *dare* you show yourself?" she screeched. Alicia was beautiful, but sadly clichéd. "You have convinced the household that Van sullied you, when we both know that you have lured him on for six months. My *husband.* How could you?"

Mary strode swiftly toward her. She had no desire for Alicia to use her penetrating voice to air her grievances.

"Alicia—Mrs. Van Allen, let me once and for all set the record straight. I have repeatedly told your husband that I want nothing amorous to do with him whether he was married or single. *He* finagled the invitation to this house party, not me. And *he* encouraged me to stay with you in London, telling me that you were having trouble finding your feet as a young matron in society. He asked me to be a friend to you. I ought to have left sooner, but I did not realize the extent of his idiocy."

Alicia glared at her, though tears rose in her round eyes. "He would never *insult* me so! As if I have not been the toast of every ball of note even after my marriage. 'Find my feet!' What nonsense."

Mary shook her head. Alicia would not be convinced by her. Probably only painful years of loneliness would teach her the truth. Mary felt genuinely sorry for her.

Still... "The barrel?" Mary asked. "Was that you?"

Alicia's look turned saucy. "With doors being locked in every direction, I took a page from the ghost's book. No one thought I'd venture outside in the snow, no one even questioned it."

Mary slid her hand around the polished knob at the top of the banister. "That explains it. I thought that barrel too heavy for the children, and the result too cruel."

"Cruel? I wish you'd frozen to death!" Even Alicia looked startled by what she'd said. She jerked her head at Colonel Fitzwilliam, who'd just come up behind Mary. "But I knew Colonel Fitzwilliam was there. I bet he kept you *warm*—"

"That's enough," he said firmly. "We make every allowance for you, but that was a childish and unhandsome prank."

"I only wanted her to get a little cold, and for Van to see what a *trollop* she is. When—"

Mary started down the stairs after the footman, who was waiting at the bottom and clearly trying to act as if he wasn't listening to every word. "No lasting harm was done. Don't start another speech."

Mary steeled herself as she went down the stairs. Alicia could not help ringing a peal over her head, as comprehensive and full of vitriol as it was full of bitterness and disappointment. Alicia was deaf even to Colonel Fitzwilliam's protests.

Thankfully Alicia was interrupted at the bottom of the stairs by her husband. Van looked sullenly at Mary but said not a word. The other gentlemen must have put the fear of God into him last night, as the saying went. He only wrapped an arm around Alicia's shoulders. "Come, my dear, the carriage is ready."

She leaned her head on his shoulder. "Oh, good. Now we may be comfortable!"

"Yes, my pet. Just say a civil goodbye to Miss Crawford and the colonel. It is good of them to see us off."

Mary scoffed. "I didn't come to see you off. I'm going for a walk on this beautiful morning." She was dressed in her cherry red velvet pelisse and had on her riding boots, quite ready for a walk. Colonel Fitzwilliam was not part of her plan, but she made use of his presence.

"Colonel Fitzwilliam was going to accompany me."

"Yes, thank you for coming down promptly." He held out his arm and she took it with a quick, beaming smile at him. They exited ahead of the Van Allens, went down the shallow steps, and skirted around the carriage, which was indeed waiting on the gravel walk.

The sun had come out in force today, and the snow only lingered in shady patches. Colonel Fitzwilliam directed their steps down the drive and toward a pleasant-looking walk that led into the trees on the south side of the house. Mary had not been on this path before, as the snow had so quickly rendered the outdoors difficult.

"This is one of the best places to walk in Pemberley," he said. "I'm glad you'll get to see it before you go. Shall I double back and have Isabella or Mrs. Knightley accompany us?"

Mary listened as the shout of the driver, the huff of horses, and the crunch of the wheels told her that the Van Allens were on their way.

"We needn't walk at all," she said. "You don't have your great coat and were not prepared for it. Thank you for playing along with my small scene."

"My pleasure. If you want to walk, I should like to. I rarely get the chance for a peaceful ramble around Pemberley. As much as I enjoy the Gardiner children, they are not peaceful."

"No, they are not."

By tacit agreement, they did not discuss the Van Allens, the tar barrel, the previous midnight, or anything unpleasant. They discussed some of their favorite parks in London— Regent's vs. Green—a concert that Mary had recently seen, and an opera that Fitz had attended in a rented box.

"I'm not much in the opera line, but my mother was determined to see it. Ghastly tragedy. One can never be sure, but I think all but the last fellow died."

"You prefer the mundane to the tragic."

"Generally. I don't mind a comedy, either."

"I had nearly forgotten! You did great justice to one of Shakespeare's popular comedies."

The play the previous evening was still uneasy ground. He pivoted away from it again, asking about her plans for the rest of winter and spring. While doing so, he pointed out some of the good vistas into the trees, and where Lizzy was teasing Darcy to add a folly.

"Does she like ruins?" Mary asked. "I wouldn't have guessed that she would want a fake Greek temple or toppled Roman chapel."

"She does it merely to amuse herself and tease Darcy. She suggested an Egyptian sphinx and his face was a picture. He never wants to directly contradict her, so he tried to subdue his horror. It was like stifling a violent sneeze."

"The poor man."

"Yes. If he had not a grand estate, loving wife, and affectionate sister, I should greatly pity him."

Mary laughed. "Pity is such a lowering thing, I only lavish it on those I dislike. Then I may feel noble that I pity my enemies, and I avoid the discomfort of insulting my friends with it. Is there not something about coal upon heads?"

"I don't know that pity is so bad. It moves us to do good things; to help when we might ignore, or to have compassion when we might criticize. I can't believe you don't believe in pity; you are too kind for that."

"No, you don't understand the beauty of my dichotomy! When there is someone I like, admire, or even tolerate, I can show them kindness out of sincerity. When there is someone I detest, I can show them kindness out of pity. It is an unassailable logical construct."

"I'd venture to say it's not, but that would not be very kind, would it? I daresay you could construct *that* into another argumentative fortress."

They were quiet as they went up a slightly steeper incline. Rough steps were cut into the ground, buttressed by logs, and made slippery with snowmelt. There were large puffy clouds that sometimes eclipsed the sun, but the sky beyond was a glorious blue. Most of the trees in this portion of the wood were pine, and their needles cast a fine fragrance as they were crushed under their boots.

At the top, they looked down onto a farther dell. It was wooded with a few open spaces, and two small ponds that could be seen half tucked into foliage. In the farther distance were some of the famed mountains of the Peak District.

"A remarkable view," Mary said. "In general, buildings give me more pleasure than mountains, and a perfect ballroom gives me more chills than a cliff—but I can see why this area is loved."

"Do not let Lizzy hear you say so. She might love these rocks and trees more than Darcy."

Mary laughed again. "This has been delightful. Thank you for the distraction."

They turned back, navigating the steps a little more slowly. He took her hand to help her step down with care. "I have more distraction if you'd like. Whatever you need."

"Whatever I need? You shouldn't offer a *carte blanche* to a woman you don't know very well."

He paused to look back at her. He was a step down, and she saw his fair cheeks redden at her words. A *carte blanche* meant merely an open offer, but its connotation was less proper. She hadn't premeditated the play on words, but it had slipped out.

"I think I do know you fairly well, Miss Crawford. I trust you won't take advantage of me."

Her eyes danced. "Oh, touché. That's taught me a lesson."

His eyes warmed. Mary felt sure he was about to kiss her. She had realized—during the rest of her long, restless night—that she had fallen in love with Colonel Fitzwilliam. He was a younger son, but what did that matter when she had wealth? He was firm and almost bourgeois in his morals, but he had believed her when it counted. In addition to all that, he was funny and witty, a joy to be around, and a loyal son and brother.

At some point, younger sons had become her type and there was nothing she could do about it.

However, while she was anticipating the warmth of his arms around her, he turned away abruptly. "This patch is all mud, take care."

Mary almost tripped in surprise.

He talked of other things on the way back. He slightly touched on the troubles of the morning, by accident merely, but Mary was done ignoring it all.

"Alicia was irate because you called her childish," Mary explained. "It is the worst adjective she knows at present."

He curled his lip. "I do pity her, but I cannot forget her ridiculous diatribe. I suppose it is good she confessed about the garden, and we did not blame that part on the children."

"See, you pity her because you do not like her," Mary pointed out gleefully.

He kicked away a pine branch that had fallen in their path. "You gloat whenever you win, I see. It is not merely in whist or backgammon."

"Gloat? Never." A cloud came over the sun, cooling the green and gray of the woods.

"Are you also a sore loser?"

"I don't lose often enough to have a pattern." She stopped him. "Colonel Fitzwilliam, I'm not made of glass. You don't need to handle me with kid gloves."

"I wasn't aware I was doing so."

"You're terrible at lying."

"I know." He ran a hand through his hair and shifted his weight. "What else can I honorably do, Miss Crawford? You need time to recover."

"I do, and I shall have it, but the two things are not mutually exclusive. I believe we were interrupted too soon in the garden. You were going to say something."

A flare of hope kindled in his face. "You told me to stop."

"I'm not telling you that now. Quite the opposite."

He began to smile. "Miss Crawford, I find that I can think of no one but you. If you don't wish me to make a foolish and sentimental speech, you ought to stop me now."

She shook her head.

He smiled a little wider. "First, it was your laughter. Then your beauty, your kindness, and your bravery."

"You forgot how intelligent and poised I am," she whispered. "That is very important to me."

"Do wait, ma'am, I am telling this. Somewhere after beauty and before kindness I noticed how clever your mind is and how quick your tongue. After kindness, I believe I noticed your exquisite ability with the harp."

"A thousand women play the harp."

He took her hand. "Not like you."

Mary looked at their hands. "You still haven't mentioned poise."

"Because I don't care about it." He cupped Mary's cheek in his hand. His thumb stroked her soft, cold skin. "Would you do me the incredible honor of accepting my hand in marriage?"

"Yes, I would." Mary usually hid her innermost emotions in sarcasm and wit, even from herself. She was startled to feel tears on her cheeks. She took a ragged breath. "Heavens above, I never do this."

He wiped them with his thumbs. "You've had a long week. Perhaps it is that. Have I rushed you? I want to protect and serve you, to spend every moment making up for what you've endured, but I can wait for you. Whatever you need."

"I have had a very long week, a very long month... an interminable year altogether. Let's not make it any longer."

Fitz finally ducked his head—the man was absurdly tall—and pressed his lips to hers.

"You're always so cold," he murmured.

Mary felt light-headed. "As I said, that's not something even wealth can prevent."

"That's because it's not the job of wealth. It's the job of a husband who loves you."

He pulled her closer, wrapping his arms around her as he'd done before, and Mary finally knew what it felt like when a heroine melted into her hero's arms.

{ 22 }

DARCY STARED AT HIS COUSIN, who was grinning like an eighteen-year-old lieutenant, not a colonel of more than thirty years. Lizzy was in his usual upholstered chair. Darcy leaned against it, taking her hand. "You did what?"

"I proposed to Miss Crawford. She accepted me."

Lizzy bounced in her seat. "I am so happy. You are exactly right; you will be very good for one another."

"He is exactly right?" Darcy repeated. "The poor girl has had a terrible week. Perhaps she ought not make a serious decision just yet. I would certainly counsel against it."

"If you were her brother or father, perhaps you should. Or if it were some gentlemen other than Fitz—but you know he is completely to be trusted! It is not as if she is being imprudent."

"I think she is."

Fitz was still grinning. "Thank you for the compliment."

"I know I haven't any authority in the matter," Darcy said, "but I am uneasy. Besides, this is what the children were trying to do, wasn't it? Do you think it wise to reward such behavior?"

Now Lizzy and Fitz were both laughing. He slapped Darcy's shoulder. "Clearly I should refuse to marry the woman I love in order to teach the children a lesson. My duty is plain."

Darcy glared at both of them. "You know what I mean. You could wait."

"I could, but I don't want to. Nor does Miss Crawford."

"You could announce your engagement at the ball tonight," Lizzy suggested.

Darcy looked his betrayal at her.

"I support you in all things, my dear sir," said Lizzy, "but this is too delicious."

Darcy threw up a hand. "Fine. Like I said, it is not as if I have any say."

"I know that galls you to admit, and I love you the better for it." Lizzy kissed his cheek.

Lady Matlock crowed when she was told of the engagement. "Oh, Fitz, you are the best of sons! Miss Crawford is every inch the lady, she is Isabella's friend, and she is a woman of substance. You have done *very* well. I am almost resigned to Harold's perpetual bachelordom."

Harold yawned when Fitz told him of the engagement. "Did I not say so? You really ought to listen to me."

Maggie and Eleanor made their sincere apologies to Miss Crawford in the nursery. They both begged pardon quite prettily, and with much sincere sorrow that it had "gotten out of hand." Their tone slipped a little at the end.

"Is it true that you are engaged to Uncle Fitz?" Eleanor asked, after blowing her nose one last time and wiping her eyes. "Bertie says he heard it from the footman who helped them dress."

Mrs. Gardiner stood. "Eleanor! That is not a proper question from a girl to a lady."

"I know. It's just—I *do* feel bad about what I did, but this would make it just the *tiniest* bit less awful."

Mary smiled. "It is true. We are engaged."

"But," Mrs. Gardiner emphasized. "Such a thing would have happened on its own. All you did with your interference was annoy your friends and endanger their visit."

"Yes, Mama," they both answered.

A stout and persistent knocking at the door heralded the entrance of Bertie and Pip.

"I have something to confess," Bertie said. "You thought it was all the girls' doing—but I kicked the ladder down. I trapped Mr. Van Allen in the attic. I even made a ghost noise to frighten him."

Mary laughed.

"Bertie!" Mrs. Gardiner pressed a hand to her forehead. She was not entirely innocent in the escapade either, so she only shook her head. "That was very naughty. No dessert for you tonight either."

"Yes, Mama."

Mary assuaged her conscience—and won three undying hearts—when she caused several desserts to be saved from the ball for her young friends the following day.

The ball itself was enjoyable. Mary did not end up being much help to Lizzy at all, but the Pemberley servants were so well conducted and independent, and Lizzy's manners such a happy mix of cheer and confidence, that it went off with barely a hitch.

Mary had the enjoyment of dancing with Fitz several times in the evening. An engaged couple could dance more than once, after all.

Mr. Holbrook and Mr. Hawksley, as well as Mr. Darcy and Mr. Knightley, also took pains to dance with her. Mr. Knightley gave her some very good advice on the tone to take in the future with Mr. Van Allen. Mr. Darcy did not speak of the matter, but by his exquisite politeness he conveyed his support. He could be rather intimidating when he was silent. Mary wished Lizzy joy of him.

Neither Mr. Holbrook nor Mr. Hawksley said a word about the previous evening either, but by their deference and perfect manners, she gathered that Mr. Darcy had spoken with them. She read correctly into their demeanor that they had no intention of speaking ill of her in the future.

Mr. Holbrook, intriguingly, was distracted when Isabella danced by with her brother Harold, who had bestirred himself to dance, much to everyone's surprise. Mr.

Holbrook danced with Georgiana twice, but it was Isabella who drew his eyes.

Harry Hawksley did not seem to have eyes for anyone in particular, but he was always a genial favorite. *He* might forget and gab about her. Mary had some doubts about him, but at least she would be a married woman. There was far greater security in that state.

Fitz noticed when that thought crossed her mind. "Why the frown, Mary? Are you tired?" He had just brought her a glass of negus, a tart mixture of port, sugar, and lemon, and he pressed it into her hand.

She took a sip. "I had the most prosaic and depressing thought about why we should get married, and I am annoyed with myself for it. There is no annoyance like realizing your path will please people you dislike."

"There *are* a number of prosaic reasons why we are perfect for one another. Perhaps I should make a list so that you can check them off as they occur to you."

"No, out with it. I hate living in suspense. Give me the worst at once."

"You drink and replenish yourself, I'll enumerate."

Mary knew her sleepless night—proceeded by several weeks of poor sleep—was doing nothing for her eyes. He was rightfully concerned. She drank.

"First, your uncle is an admiral, and I am a colonel. There is a pleasing symmetry, even though the British Navy can never equal our forces on land."

She smiled. "That's debatable but continue."

"I prefer to live in London; you also like London."

"I do. That one is not so bad."

"At times I'll help Darcy with estate duties at Pemberley and Rosings Park, or I'll help my brother at Matlock. You'll have all the country escapes you could want."

"That's pastoral, not prosaic."

"True. How about this." He winced. "I am a younger son, and you have a fortune."

She waved her hand. "I knew that one from the beginning."

"It does not bother you?"

"You are far from the only man who must marry a lady with some income. If I thought you had pursued me for that—but I know you did not. In fact, you were the most insulting man alive, despite my fortune."

"I was; I apologize."

"You're almost forgiven, but I shall bring the grievance back out when I need it; I am not a saint."

"I am warned. That was the last prosaic horror on my list."

She finished her sugary, lemon-laced drink. "Excellent, now I can rest easy."

He pressed her wrist. "I hope you *will* rest. You look as if you have not slept in days. You are the most beautiful, exhausted woman I have ever seen."

"I can admit that I am tired, and I will retire early. I asked Mrs. Gardiner to loan me Eleanor and Maggie tonight. Sarah has set up a pallet by the fireplace in my room. They are ever so excited, and they will be more so when they find out I saved several desserts for them."

He took her empty glass. "Are you certain two giggly little girls are what you need? That doesn't sound restful at all."

"On the contrary, Mrs. Gardiner assures me once they fall asleep they are dead to the world. It will give me pleasure and prevent any unhealthy solitude."

"Then I am glad. You will be lonely in London, however."

"I shall, but I shall contrive. The banns will only take three weeks." Suddenly she whipped her head to the edge of the ballroom nearest the door. "That's Henry. My brother!"

Colonel Fitzwilliam followed her gaze. There was a handsome gentleman in the latest town rig and curly hair in artful chaos. He looked significantly like Miss Crawford.

She skirted around to meet him, and his eyes lit up when he finally saw her among all the unfamiliar faces.

"Henry, you silly boy, what are you doing here?"

He ignored this and embraced her. "My dear Mary, have you been ill?"

"That is no way to make me feel better if I have. You must always pretend a woman looks her absolute best. Henry, this is Colonel Richard Fitzwilliam. Colonel, this is my brother, Henry Crawford."

Both men bowed, but Henry clearly wanted to shake off their company. Fitz exchanged polite greetings and left them on their own.

"Really, Henry, what are you doing here?" Mary repeated. "I thought you were going to lay low at Everingham and not leave Norfolk till March."

"My spirits could not bear it. Come away, an ugly woman is watching us. Did you think after seeing the news about Fanny and Edmund, after receiving your letter, that I could do less than see you? I am suffering my just deserts; I have enough morals to know that. But you were innocent in this—and I yelled at you when we last spoke."

"You were overwrought; I understood."

"I was, but none of it was your fault. I am sorry you lost Edmund."

Mary bit her lip.

"What does that look mean?"

"This is awkward."

"Mary."

"I'm engaged to that man you just met." She raised a hand. "I was going to write to you tomorrow; he only made his proposals today."

"What?" He laughed; he was incredulous. "That boring, overgrown officer? I know I am not in any place to judge, but—"

"No, you are *not.* You told me to stay out of your life months ago, and you have certainly stayed out of mine. You do not know what I have dealt with, what I have feared, or what I have learned."

Henry softened. He placed a gentle hand on her back. "Come tell me then. I am sorry. If you are certain, I'm sure I'll come around."

And when he had heard a tightly edited version of recent events—and had gone through all the anger, self-recrimination, and guilt she could handle—he apologized again.

"I don't want your apologies," Mary said. "But your approval would be nice."

Henry made a face as he studied Colonel Fitzwilliam across the room.

"Don't call him boring," Mary warned him. "You said the same thing about Fanny."

"That is not fair."

"I don't care."

They studied one another, complete understanding passing between them, as it did when they were young. They were not twins, but their upbringing had all but made them so. "You're different," Henry said simply.

"Yes, I am."

"Very well. Introduce me to all these relations you are soon to have."

Mary did make a circuit of introductions, introducing Henry as her brother. He apologized multiple times for coming to the ball uninvited. He asserted that as Mary gave him the date and he was traveling through the neighborhood, he could not resist.

Mary wasn't sure this would have been enough under other circumstances. The Darcy family knew of his affair with Maria Rushworth and the subsequent scandal. He might not have received the cut direct, but they would have cut up stiff. As it was, however, they were eager to make amends to Mary, and it was obvious her brother was an excellent addition to her comfort.

Henry himself was surprised at his welcome. "Very decent folk, I must say. I haven't been to a party this pleasant since... before." He looked over his shoulder, a mischievous twinkle in his eye. "That last young lady, Georgiana Darcy, is she a cousin? She has rather the same air as Fanny, does she not?"

"*No*," Mary said.

"No, she's not a cousin, or—"

"Just *no*."

He smirked. "You have clearly moved on. Why shouldn't I—"

"I'm serious, Henry."

He sighed. "I'm not going to make Miss Darcy fall in love with me, I promise."

"That is better. Now, I want to talk to Colonel Fitzwilliam again, and I want you to be on your best behavior. He is not boring at all. In fact, with your dramatic reading skills and his acting ability, you are very well matched."

"Do you want me to talk to him or recite poetry?"

"Be quiet, brother, or I will step on your foot."

When Lizzy dragged herself into her room and sagged at her dressing table after the ball was over, it was nearly three in the morning. Her stoic and severe maid, Clara, waited for her.

Lizzy had told her to go to bed, but she was not surprised that Clara's duty came first. Her severe hairstyle was not a wit out of place despite the late hour. Lizzy was relieved to see her. "You are a comfort to me, I must say. I am so tired I would crawl into bed fully clothed and ruin this gown if you were not here to undress me."

"I daresay you would, ma'am." Clara deftly undid the buttons.

"My first house party has not exactly been a success, has it? With the children causing mischief—however well intentioned it might have been!—and the fiasco with poor Mary... If I even *hint* about making up a party next winter, you have my permission to give me a sharp shake."

Clara's mouth compressed.

"And I know you suspected the children sooner than I did, and I apologize for not giving your suspicions more credence. I will never doubt you again."

Clara's dark eyes narrowed skeptically.

"Well, if ever we are having a mysteriously difficult and vexatious house party, I will not doubt you. I still don't think the second housemaid is pilfering feathers from the pillows."

"Suspiciously flat, miss, suspiciously flat."

Lizzy yawned widely. "Perhaps. Oh, what a long day! After I see everyone off tomorrow and the following day, I shall sleep the clock 'round."

"You'd deserve it, miss."

"What? Clara, you've shocked me awake. What a compliment. Have you a fever? Your cheeks are pink."

Clara's jaw became even sharper than usual. "No fever. I never catch cold."

"I did not truly suspect you."

"Fact is, Mrs. Darcy..."

The use of her full name made Lizzy's eyes fly up to her ladies' maid. "Yes?"

"One of those times, it wasn't the children. I shut Mr. Van Allen in the larder." She raised her chin. "He hadn't ought to be there, poking his nose into proper servants' work."

Lizzy was in awe, having never her maid so loquacious. "No, he shouldn't."

"Felt I ought to tell you."

"Thank you, Clara." Lizzy obediently slid her arms out of the sleeves as Clara tugged at the shoulders and bodice of her dress. By the time the dress was lifted over her head and Clara had turned away to shake it, her face was as it always was—colorless and all but expressionless.

"You're a gem, Clara, I hope you know that."

"Don't pick at your hair, miss, you'll have knots for days. I'll do it properly."

Lizzy meekly submitted.

{ 23 }

MARY'S FINAL NIGHT AT PEMBERLEY was spent with two very happy little girls—who felt very grown-up to spend the night in her room. There may have been rather a lot of rustling and shifting after the final goodnight, but Mary found it surprisingly homey to hear their small noises.

They were all rather heavy-eyed the following morning, but a morning treat did wonders for their tired eyes. Eleanor hugged Mary carefully before going back to the nursery. "I am so happy for you and Uncle Fitz. Now you will not be Miss Crawford anymore, you will be Aunt Mary!"

This was startling, as *Aunt Mary* sounded like an old woman with chilblains and miles of tatting. Mary smiled anyway. If *she* deigned to be an Aunt Mary, she would soon make it a fashionable and popular title.

Mary's final meal at Pemberley was spent with her brother and her fiancé. Henry and Fitz were not on the best of terms, but they were civil. Henry had too much to atone for and though Mary knew he recognized his errors, his manner was always light and humorous. It did not give much insight into his mind. As much as she loved her brother, she was thankful to marry someone quite different.

The two happiest couples of the house were nearby—Knightley and Emma, Darcy and Lizzy—but this time Mary's heart did not ache when she glanced at their foursome. She was no longer separated by a glass pane from the warmth of their family, and that made all the difference.

When she rode back to London with Lady Matlock and Isabella, she was now a future daughter and sister. This did not save her from a lengthy lecture on the themes of Goethe's latest work translated from German, or from Lady Matlock's speculations about the most efficient timeline of future grandchildren, but it gave both a charm that was new to Mary. That of female family.

She had also received, at the last moment, another invitation for the following Christmas.

"You and Fitz are always welcome," Lizzy said. "That is, if we ever attempt to host a house party again. Mr. Darcy and I agree this one was a catastrophe."

"Any subsequent attempts must go better then, if we go by probabilities," Mary said.

"Or Pemberley will be burnt to the ground," Lizzy said dryly. "Or swallowed in an earthquake."

Mr. Darcy turned from his conversation. "What's that?"

"Nothing, my dear." Lizzy grinned. "I was only trying to get Miss Crawford's support for my Egyptian folly in the home wood."

He made a face quite like a repressed sneeze. "Ah. Of course."

Mary tapped Fitz's arm. "You described him to a tee."

"I am a clever fellow."

Mr. Knightley cleared his throat. "Perhaps you would all consider visiting Hartfield next Christmas. Emma and I would be pleased to have you."

This was agreed to as heartily as tentative plans made for a year in advance could be.

Emma beamed at them all. "Yes, next year we'll welcome the new year from Hartfield. Hopefully!"

The End

Character List

NAME, TITLE (ROLE IN *MUCH ADO*)

Mrs. Elizabeth Darcy

Mr. Fitzwilliam Darcy

Mrs. Sophia Fitzwilliam, Lady Matlock (technically Dowager Lady Matlock)

Mr. Harold Fitzwilliam, Lord Matlock

Colonel Richard Fitzwilliam (Benedick)

Miss Isabella Fitzwilliam (Don John/Beatrice)

Mr. Edward Gardiner (Borachio)

Mrs. Madeleine Gardiner

Margaret "Maggie" Gardiner, 11 (the nurse)

Eleanor Gardiner, 9 (the maid)

Bertrand "Bertie" Gardiner, 8 (Dogberry)

Phillip "Pip" Gardiner, 6 (Friar Francis)

Miss Mary Crawford (Beatrice/ Don John)

Mr. Thomas "Van" Van Allen (Don Pedro)

Mrs. Alicia Van Allen (Hero)

Mr. Harry Hawksley (Claudio)

Mr. Adam Holbrook (several small roles)

Mr. George Knightley (Antonio)

Mrs. Emma Knightley (Leonato)

Other Books by Corrie Garrett

An Austen Ensemble Series
A Lively Companion
A True Likeness
A Gentle Touch

The Highbury Variation
From Highbury with Love
From London with Loyalty
From Pemberley with Luck

Sweet Regency Saga, the Persuasion Variation
Starch and Strategy
Propriety and Piquet

Stand-alone and Modern Variations
Pride and Prejudice and Passports
The Rise and Fall of Jane
One Winter's Ball

ABOUT THE AUTHOR

CORRIE GARRETT has worked an array of jobs from pet grooming and English instruction, to office support at aerospace research laboratories and highway construction offices. Now she has the oddest job of all, writing historical romances and speculative fiction! From the finer points of historical opium to chemical explosives, her google search history probably confuses the government algorithms meant to track us all. She lives and works in West Virginia with her husband and four children, and she enjoys writing hopeful fiction of family and faith.

For more information on books, series, and new releases visit her website at www.corriegarrett.com. Or come say hello through her Facebook page at Corrie Garrett, Author!

Made in the USA
Las Vegas, NV
22 December 2023